THE LAST BEATNIK

Frank Palescandolo

iUniverse, Inc.
New York   Bloomington

The Last Beatnik

Copyright © 2010 Frank Palescandolo

iUniverse books may be ordered through booksellers or by contacting:

iUniverse
1663 Liberty Drive
Bloomington, IN 47403
www.iuniverse.com
1-800-Authors (1-800-288-4677)

ISBN: 978-1-4401-7554-1 (pbk)
ISBN: 978-1-4401-7555-8 (ebk)

Printed in the United States of America

iUniverse rev. date: 11/9/2010

Author's Note

The novel was suggested also by the life and art of the Russian painter Nicholas Roerich whose paintings are collected privately and in worldwide museums, and the Nicholas Roerich Museum in New York City.

Unspeakable colors! Ranging like the canvases of Nicholas Roerich. Rays transparent through earth's atmosphere horizon becoming orange, gradually turning into rainbow colors, blue, dark blue, purple, black.

Gagarin, cosmonaut

The Wanderer

I am a wanderer, he said to his heart, and a mountain-climber. I am no lover of the plains and it seems I cannot sit still for long.

And what is still to come by way of fate and experience, it will include wandering and climbing mountains. In the end, a man's experience is only himself.

The time has passed when accidents could still befall me and what could happen to me that is not already mine?

It only returns, finally comes home to me – my own self – and what long faraway places, scattered among things and events.

And I know something else now standing in front of my highest peak, the one that has waited for me the longest time. Oh! I must start the hardest of my journey, begin the loneliest of my wanderings.

But one who is like me cannot escape this moment. The moment that tells him, now at last you are on your way to greatness. Mountain-tops and valleys are joined together.

Zarathrusta
Friedrich
Neitzche

Happenings

You Don't Have to Die in Benares

My name is George Dreyfus. I am owner of a book store in downtown Brooklyn, not far from the Municipal Building on Borough Square. Why do I mention my nearness to the Municipal Building? Because this is where a narrative begins, not mine but that of a poorly identified man who left books fifty years ago in a hotel room on Montague Street, intestate. Intestate, this is where I come in. In the basement there was a spare room that was used to auction off belongings of a person who died without a will and known relatives. Under the laws of New York state, such belongings, clothes, furniture, money, bric-a-brac and books, this is where I come in again, were sold at public auction and proceeds were turned over to the state treasury. Books. Whenever books were part of appropriation by the State, I was called to set a value on the books before auction time. On a wintry March afternoon, I got the call from the manager of this special unit of intestate auctioneers attached to the Surrogate's Court, to place values on a collection of books. I told my clerk to take over the store while I headed in a patchy snowstorm to the Municipal Building where I took the elevator to the basement floor. I was led to a corner of a large boiler-like room to view the books of the missing man. I was immediately intrigued by the titles of frayed books authored by Jack Kerouac, Allan Ginsberg, William Burroughs, Neal Cassaday and others known to me. All were first editions and inscribed cursorily to the late "Beatniks."

"Hey!" I held the book-like posters. "The guy like the rest, was a Beatnik!"

1

"But that's all we were able to find out," replied the worker from behind a rack upon which stood a can of rusted paint and a shriveled brush.

"According to the inscriptions in these books he was not a nothing. He knew the writers of the Beat generation. Must have been have been a contemporary, or on the margin. Bookwise, I am I can't identify this stranger," I said.

At that moment, the supervisor Joe Martino appeared.

"Did you set a price, Dreyfus?"

"The 173 books have real value, Tom. This loner contains autographs and all are first editions. Each is worth hundreds of dollars."

"Give me a bottom price. The auction of loners begins tomorrow morning, right here."

"They should be advertised as notice first to collectors for a better price. Paste it on your store window. You get browsers every day."

"I'll do that. I'll be one of the bidders, Tom."

Tom smiled. "Then you set a low starting bid."

"I can't do that!"

"Suit yourself, then."

"I would begin at 200 dollars each."

"May I take them with me until tomorrow?"

"All? Sorry, I can't bend the rules."

Back in his book shop on the last day of an historic career as a place to meet up and coming writers of the Fifties and Sixties, to taste the wide literary culture and taste of the proprietor. George rose and fell with the downfall of the Beats stretched over the years on the longest and most eye-catching shelf below the cupboard where all the hash was cached by the Dharma Bums, Naked Angels, Beatniks, Bohemian Bums, or simply bums. George never had a title on that shelf, although he had a share of the hashish and booze in the cupboard. He had been a NT, a non-talent member of the Beats. Why didn't he tell Tom Martino of his identity with the Beats? Was he ashamed? Hell! no! Proud? Yes!

After fifty years, the ruin of the Beats hurt him deeply, he saw their end and his end the partly demolished shop of his creation.

This was his last day, their day was past, but not his memory, sharpened by the phantom of an unknown Beatnik, the living presence of the books all serried like DNA fixed, in his mind to unconquerable youth. His doorway was gone! A last dog crapped on his large window sill, the seat of tomes of Nobel Prize Winners, George choked with milled dust in a site that once was as fragrant as a seraglio with strong scents of perfume, absinthe and crème de menthe mixes and sweet sex.

A lengthy, liveried Lincoln Cabriolet scraped the crumbling curb of the store. A chauffeur alighted, walked to the passenger side and slowly opened the door wide for an elderly lady who leveraged herself with a can and arm of her chauffeur. Familiar with the anatomy of the book shop, she stepped down the three steps from the street level to the lower level occupied by a rented tin sheeted table at which Dreyfus corpulently sat. He looked up dim-sighted, curious, then turned to papers on his table he was annotating. He figured she was a dotty lady who lost her way and imagine this to be a milliner's shop of a half-century ago. He was being evicted that day, that afternoon at three. He expected no visitors. Nothing on display in his speckled window of fly shit. Out of business, out of mind.

The lady visitor stumbled, alarming Dreyfus, all that was needed today to make it Black Friday was a lawsuit during a demolition. He rushed to her side tipping his chair. She waved him away with the cane, pointed at his belly and moved him back to his small alcove.

In a cracked voice she said, "You never were of any use George."

"I? Madam, do I know you?"

"I know you George. You were always old."

"Madam! who are you?"

"Come on, George. I don't look that bad, new wig, just had a facial."

She permitted him to move closer to her face, although she squirmed with some embarrassment.

Dreyfus softened his eyes, stroked his whiskered chin. Was it? Could be? That greenish shine still in her mascaraed eyes. The same frame of a once shapely woman, the sweetheart, the flower girl of the Beats. "Is that you, Susan Appleton?"

"At last! Did you need an autopsy?"

"Oh Susan!" tears came to his eyes. You will always be a lovely woman. These eyes of mine!"

"Well, I forgive those rheumy eyes, old friend"

He hugged her gently, he found her so frail. He kept repeating "Susan Appleton. Susan Appleton."

"If you bring one tear to my eyes, my makeup collapses and I shall beat you with my cane." She smiled and placed her wrinkled left hand on his.

"Ah! George you were always such a bore, your head in books, squinting like a mole. You never said anything, or did anything original like the Beats."

"Ah! Susan, you love them, not me, they were something special."

"You mean quirky geniuses?"

"I'll buy that with spades!"

"You got something to drink in this dreary place. Cognac?"

His face wrinkled. "Susan, we never heard of cognac in those days. It was all straight and bottoms up, cheap wine, gin, rum, and the heaps of hashish in that corner cupboard."

Susan turned to her chauffeur still standing by. "Raoul, fetch the rest of the cognac." And he did, with two brandy glasses. He filled them and served them to George and Susan. No bottoms up, they sipped warily.

"George, you are too stupid to ask. What are we drinking to?"

"Our reunion, of course."

"Don't flatter yourself."

"So – you came to flirt at last, to make up for those years of indifference to me." He performed a Hamlet gesture.

She luffed a bit of laughter and pursed her lip.

He said sniffing the lees of the cognac. "Susan, be kind –"

"George, I am speaking of the reunion lovingly, and of course that includes you. So don't sniffle in my brandy glasses."

"I am not sniffling–"

"I am back."

"Ah! You saw the notice in the City Register?" The books!

"I am here to talk about business."

George needed another drink. What a day! He extended his glass to Raoul, who obeyed her signal and returned the bottle to the limo instead.

"You have discovered more than a hundred first editions of the Beats signed and genuine?"

"Yes, in great condition. I vouched for every item. My official imprimatur is as appraiser for the Surrogate's Court."

"You don't need a title. You are the grandpere of the Beats."

"Nice of you to say that, Susan."

"Don't you dare say I am a grandmere. That would be a howl!"

"You slept with all of them."

"Still jealous, not all. There are some who – well, anyway, you are auctioning off the lot and set a bidding price."

"Yes. It's all set for tomorrow at ten. Booksellers from all over the country will be there. I have been busy making hotel arrangements for those cutthroats."

"I make it easy for you. I shall buy all of them, every single one of them at the highest bid."

"That's a lot of money, Susan. It will cost you about ten thousand, at least."

"And your commission."

"I'll buy a cabana in Florida."

"George in the spirit of this meeting and old times sake, I'll give you a bungalow on the Gulf side which I never use. Too stormy."

She paused.

"If you auctioned them off the volumes would be scattered, lost, misplaced, and neglected after fifty years. Yes, my dear boys deserve a monument. You will notice there has been awareness in Jack, Neal and Larry and the rest George. They died so young, so badly, drink, drugs self-destruction. When you love something, it spites you, they loved life and it spited them with bad fortune.

"I agree, Susan, I mourn them in my own way, alone in the shop where I still hear Allan descanting. Jack singing, Cassady doing an impromptu and —"

"Yes. Yes. George don't get maudlin, let's get down to business, for I have become a business woman per force."

"Per force? What are you talking about?"

"First, are the books mine?"

"Yes. Where will I deliver them to?"

"Columbia University. It's okay with them."

"And the bungalow?"

"Raoul will bring the deed tomorrow at the auction and a check for old time's sake."

"Now Susan I must tell how happy you have made me this day but of all the girl Beats I loved you truly. There hasn't been a day when I have not thought of you, worried about what happened to you, where you were."

"You did not recognize me. George."

"You must remember Susan. You are my flower girl."

"George! George! You improved your manners. You were such a bore then."

She righted a fluff of hair on her brow, "Most of the girls as you might know went blewie, worse than the boys, a disaster. You are the only one left."

"Another."

"This lad who left the books in the hotel room. Who was he?"

"We don't know, the assumption is he is dead. The auction only evidence was a can of pigment cans and a paint brush. And yes, an easel."

"If he was a Beat, I do not recall him. I knew of no such Beat who was a painter, and yet — a person comes to my mind, hanger on. Serious, thick red hair, inward look, lanky. He was the only one who said no to me. Maybe that's why I remember so well."

"I am sure if he had lived he would be famous today. All the Beats were extraordinarily talented. And if he is living, George would be the last Beatnik. I was only an NT like you."

"You said business, a talent for business."

"Not even that George. Like the other girls I went blewie too. Parents fixed me up in a drying out institute in Connecticut. Very posh. Electroshock, all the rest. An elderly gentleman was there too as a patient. Elderly, he was only in his sixties. He took a liking to me and I to him. What relationship, I am not sure to this day. I think he always wanted a daughter, and he found me. In him I found support in the end that helped him. So we both recovered. We had a good life. He died. I am a rich old lady, who might still be in love with a lanky Beat who was a painter, who did not give a hoot for me."

"Well Susan, he did not deserve your burning flesh. You did not monumentalize him in your gift for as far as I know he was not a lonely painter, not a word!"

"A painter you said?"

"Signs of it."

"Goodbye George."

"Goodbye Susan. Watch your step."

"Not too subtle."

George Dreyfus' funny mustache drooping when police digged him about the hashish cached on the premises. All the girls bodies soaked with Chanel Oriental emollients to give them sexual appeal which they paraded openly with slit dresses. And ooo! The vomiting in corners and pissing in dark corners, a playpen of undiapered children, Corso and Larry signing up putative writers who called themselves the Beats who would never write a line worth a nickel. Young professors from Columbia standing by, too timid to join, playing den mothers to unruly flock. In later years they claimed rapid academic papers and early publication. The discovery of these few talented kids was like something found under a rock.

Lights flickered, dimming. Edison's warning, perhaps now he would have a chance to read more carefully easel, paint pot and brush left behind by the young Beatnik years ago at the now defunct Montague Hotel. The police had no use for them, hardly enough for a John Doe entry. No proof of death. The coroner, annoyed by such trivial matter, left early from the scene. In hand were not testamentary papers when examined by a City lawyer. A suspicion, a lingering loss of faith with Beatniks, another writer at Bellevue. Depending on how you arranged, he either killed himself or finally ended up in a State asylum as did the others.

The Fifties

ANTHONY CURTIS, ADOPTED SON of the Divine of St. John's church on the Plymouth Heights of Brooklyn, not far from the bookstore of George Dreyfus on Montague Street. He was the illegitimate child of a Trumbull lady from the eminent Trumbull family, a long line of Congregationalist adherents running back to Emerson. The Divine and his wife were childless and welcomed the unwanted infant into the larger congregational circle of great preachers and intellectuals. But the Divine was modern, realized that the boy if he became a distinguished and leading member of the affiliate congregations would have some knowledge of the secular ways of the new world outside the precincts of the Plymouth Church in Brooklyn. He enrolled him at Columbia University of which he was a trustee. Grades at Columbia were not exceptional; he got a gentleman C's. He spent a kind of wayward student life away from the actual campus. From early morning on the train to Brooklyn, he painted and sketched the nascent beauty of Morningside Heights Park or did portraits of blacks from nearby Harlem. Nevertheless he was admired by the parishioners of his elegant presence, an inner dignity, courteous to a fault, so handsome in his white surkice, red headed and tousled. At sixteen, over six feet, a gangly body with a marked stoop on his right shoulder which was his brush arm. He had a baritonal voice that sounded beautifully off the coffered oak ceilings.

What would they think of him now. Out of Bellevue, his faith broken in his ancestral church, disillusioned and sick by the antics of the

Beatniks, of which he considered himself a member in its jejune beliefs. No, he could not face his betters, the Divine and his wife.

It happened so, after a night of orgy, not planned, a self-generating momentum, a nightlong round of boozing, cannabis and cocaine. Orgiastic in all ways, an entangled mass of naked bodies slovenly drunk with heavenly highs, so they said. All mouthing aums free of pricks and cunts, chanting Eastern hymns of which they had only a dim understanding. The knot of Beats was joined here, and there, by the innocent and curious living in the rundown tenement. A professor and several instructors at Columbia University joined at the edges timidly smoking hashish, red eyed, and dozing. I was among them, a spectator looking on an arena of sexual acrobats, while a distance fell between us. Did my Third Eye suddenly open, just then? None of us had any elemental notion of the grand cosmic insights of the religions of the East. I saw my Beat Buddies playing with dangerous toys. Playing jacks with rounded spheres which rolled off the table. I withdrew into myself like a mollusk backing into his shell. I, like the others, once smug in the arms of fakirism, and imbecilities which prompted the indecencies I was witnessing. My heart cried: Impure! Impure! I imagined only days ago with the Beats, I was free of existential cares. What I was experiencing now was a genuine religious crisis, some might say! But that description would only dignify a state of sheer anxiety and shitty panic. I rose, my limbs trembling with fear, I must flee, where, and what from? I fled the room toppling nearby joiners in my haste, I vaulted the staircases five flights down, careened into the misty darkness of early daybreak. I ran a rabid dog through the streets of Upper Broadway, and into the gloom. Before a stoop, I fell sprawling, exhausted, foam at my lips. Fingers plucked at my body until I was stark naked on the cold pavement. I passed out.

I mourned the early deaths of my Beat comrades of the Fifties: Ginsberg, Kerouac, Cassady. The mourning from a distance of some years after I realized that the Beat road was a nether road of self-exploitation of drugs and booze closing on an ending of buffoonery and tragic farce. How young we were, all hoping to open the Third Eye while experiencing only a spiritual bemusement and hokey simple-mindedness at the feet of religious teachers of the East. We called ourselves Desolation Angels. No one knew what dharma meant in the canons of Buddha and Yoga. No Dioynisian exhaltation, only opportunistic sex. I moved away from the company, never judging them as I abandoned friendships I still respect. Behind all shenanigans there existed a religious fervor that struggled for expression and consummation and substantial talent. Parting from my Bums of the Beat World was not a firm decision after deep thought; it was an act of suicide. My suicide. I cut my wrists, not deep enough so I awakened in a deep faint, configured by blood. I smelled self-slaughter. And why? Why? I was twenty six years of age, a Flower Child. Then I vowed to love my life, take me where it wills, do me what it wills, Amor Fati, it was not my life that mattered. It was life that mattered. Life!

Bellevue

WHEN I WAS TAKEN to Bellevue Psychiatric Ward I was in a state of severe depression. I huddled within myself, bone against bone, trying to discover surcease in a living center of dead and numbing feeling. I remained in this condition for weeks and more until one bright afternoon. I was sitting on a pavilion chair facing the East River swaddled in a gray blanket that swaddled my eyes. A blanket corner flapped open revealing to my eyes a pattern of active ants encircling a cement flower pot. I was struck by a fearless wonder. As I reached out to them lovingly, they chained across the grinning muscles of my face and prickled my face. I crossed my arms as if to embrace them all. I stood tall suddenly, the blanked fell to the pavement. I stood naked against the rusted railing of the pavilion. I was free of that clammy fear and most therapeutic of all I was told I began to sob violently that shook a once rigid body into a dawning acquiescence of that day.

I was painting to create a distance between myself and the written word of the Beats. A double view, some say the artist's irony. It is impossible to see irony in one's life without a view apart, a canvas on a distant easel. Is there a plot in my life, a prescription, a set course, a dead reckoning? Finally, I accepted the dictum of ancient source, Amor Fati. Love your life and allow it to play out its potentialities. A galvanic impulse! North. North!

The Highlands

CURTIS DID NOT OBSERVE the polarizing sun through the dense hemlock grove beginning about Rye on the Hudson River Highland. With a migratory absence of thought, he headed north along the North River, once the name of the river Hudson. Three days on the road, skirting the Taconic Highway, along the defiles, landfalls, edges of the highland, avoiding the cities and busy towns along the way. These bypaths needed signs for hot dog stands, fruit, plants, corn, squash, huge pumpkins, autumn was tailing early winter, rims of snow on the distant Catskills. His backpack of easel, paint and brushes was a light load. He stashed no food for he ate on the way to his sign jobs, where sometimes a hot dog, or a sandwich was offered. Whatever he spent of those collected dollars from Bellevue, went for paint from hardware stores or farmer's stock into cans smaller. Enough for only half the day, he painted whatever he saw of interest. And that was nothing short of the entire Hudson Valley and its great stream.

The impetus, turmoil of rapids upstream matched his own tumbled emotions on leaving his faith as a Congregationalist minister and planned destiny. Often, he dangerously climbed slippery rocks to catch the foaming force of blocked water. He found some release in the final freedom of the break through over, and between river boulders, which he painted while teetering on lichened and mossy surfaces. He wished to be scourged, not chastened. Often paintings washed out. He did not mind, the experience was the satisfaction, until later, when the artist, and not the naturalist emerged.

He arrived late at night at a clearing close to the river where he settled down for the night with a light blanket. When he opened his eyes in the morning, he was confused about where he was. He was lying in a meadow and farmland recently gleaned and fenced by white pickets.

Pathways were lined with poplars lined properly as if ruled leading into the embankment of the riverside whose scene since his position was upgrade of the river. He sighted rows of look alike farmhouses and large cottages. Of different tints, he was not sure it was the morning light that produced the hues that prettied buildings, not Currier and Ives, was more beautiful, yet prim and prosperous from the huge mounds of manure and forage that distanced the houses. It was so silent, not a bird peeped. For an instant, he thought he was dead and in a limbo of some sort or what he picked up from his fellow Beatniks, a Shambala, a secret land somewhere not heaven but terrestrial and heavenly. Then he heard the mooing of cows and he awakened to a reminiscent Dutch settlement of the highlands of the Hudson. Names and signs, Van Loon, Ruysdael, Kreisler, Steen, better, he lay there, or more meaningfully, did nothing. There was nothing to paint.

He lay there smelling the clover, snatching a straw to chew the milky fragrance of clover. Suddenly a farmer with a fork was at his side.

"You are trespassing, sir."

He faced a young woman leaning on a pitchfork. He hurried to his feet, spit out the straw, and lamely mumbled "Excuse me."

She laughed. "You apologize as if you entered a living room with manure on your shoes."

"I did not see the trespassing signs. It was dark."

"Anyway, tramps don't pay attention."

"I am not a tramp, Miss."

"I know that you are well spoken."

"I'll remove myself immediately. I'll take that path." A narrow path to her right.

She moved to block him and stood astride, her mouth teasing.

"Any why not, please?"

"Sir, in twenty yards you face an escarpment which you cannot leap and will surely fall to your death."

"It is daylight. I can see where I'm going."

"I won't allow you. All the foot bridges are now rotted. Please, sir."

"I must go."

"Where to?"

"North."

"Goodness, north is a large place."

"A general direction."

She leaned on her fork. "I see you are a sign painter. You can paint North, South, East, West anywhere you like. Nothing for you to letter here, we do ourselves."

"So I move on, thank you."

"You are a hasty young man. You know where you are?"

"Yes, in the Highlands of the Hudson Valley."

"The men wear beards here but I have not seen one as scarlet as yours. Are you Dutch?"

Across from the farmland and pastures he spied the personalized houses of the first colonists distinct by angled and the creative-looking barns, roofs or structure, the Rambler, a gambrel winter kitchen, a snug styled barn, the prominent Dutch Knuckle or creative stock lean-tos. Curtis recognized none. They rivaled in a lovely crystallization against the horizon. From afar he saw fetish hex signs of the superstitious Dutch at every crossroad, a melange of hex signs and curious symbols.

"Way back, English I guess maybe Scot."

"If you wish to trim your beard I have shears but no razors."

"Bristles keep me warm."

"I cozied under my husband's beard, not as large though, he is younger. But no one would cozy with you. You smell, not badly, the woodland smells: moss, damp and rotten wood, deer turds, yellowed fungus mushrooms."

"You don't smell yourself usually, I apologize."

"No need at all. The worse is sour milk and cheese. In the winter we bathe as a group on the Hudson riverside, although I prefer a small cataract nearby that is gentler, but colder and always spring like. I suggest you make use of it before you leave. I'll join you."

Her eyes never blinked. "You join me."

"Oh yes! We do communal bathing, no shame."

"It is not my custom!"

"Oh come! What is your name?"

"Anthony Curtis."

"We have queer customs but we are behaved. My name is Marthe."

Hudson Valley Highland Dutch girl, no doubt a Van Steen from crossroads signs and warnings, never in past remembrance did he ever focus squarely to an easel of genre painting of the Dutch School. Landscapes so still, waiting for something to happen, a harvest, a thrashing, a milling. This young lady so refreshingly forward, a delight for Curtis to study, although he had no intent to. Actual, and all pasture lines lead to her. Just above being short, stocky, fair hair and no frilly bonnet cap. Eyebrows faint as to be non-existent. Her eyes, why no Delft blue? Her stubby nose tinted in a rubicund complexion. Pretty? Yes. She looked like a lollipop. Her hands were large with tiny fingers. Was he describing a toy-like image of a girl highlander? Dairy maid? He stopped his playful descriptions. He enjoyed the overall bounce of her words, the slight Dutch accent. She was endearing.

Her lips unimaginably red like a wild carnation. His imagination went askance, at times she seemed prettily dwarfish but that was not the case. Her teeth were strong and vividly white against the strikingly red lips. She hardly walked, she bounded, lost in the woods by a careless nanny. He was convinced she was a doll as she stood still lost in the woods.

"It is not proper." Curtis for an instant, in this semi-wilderness, felt prudish.

"We are alone."

"Well, my husband, my father, Diedrick families, and the council sent me here to reconsider my ways, which Mr. Curtis, are innocent as is my offer to you."

"You are still a child in my eyes."

"Mr. Curtis, here in this dairy country babies fast siring and foals. I have seen a male before I saw myself. Dairy maids help at the whelpings. But first, a bowl of milk and for you, heavy cream and molasses. And then I scrub your beard. When I first saw you, I thought you were a stag with leaves of scarlet oak on his jaw."

"I see a cataract through the firs, it sparkles."

"It prickles you all over. Are you ready?"

"I'll meet you there."

"Don't steal away on me."

"I'll be there."

He joined her under the spring cataract, really, molten ice. She roughed his beard with a loaf of soap and cleaned his ears with short fingers. In her naked arms, Curtis thought of her as a young calf, chubby, soft skin that dimpled at the touch. She seemed to breathe milk, her bosom was large for her age, short torso and her legs could be longer.

She was pubes to pubes with him, but Curtis did not react. She made no attempt to excite him. They seemed to be enjoying an innocent playfulness. His hand felt her left breast. Curtis was curious by the size.

She slapped his hand. "Sir, you are innocent. You were wondering about my breasts which to be truthful are still lactating. I gave birth to a boy three months ago. He died. I was blamed because I insisted on riding my horse until pregnancy. Anyway, my husband's family appealed to the Council to have my marriage dissolved because of my dangerous riding that threatened the baby and future children."

"Until the council decided what to do about my reckless marriage, they sent me up here alone to consider my sin. They will return a verdict as soon as possible. My husband and I love each other and are inconsolable, although I may seem cheerful."

Curtis bowed his head in sympathy. His beard dripping lava soap. "I hope the verdict brings you together again."

"Really, Mr. Curtis, I did not mind the stay over here for almost a month. I got to thinking about many things, not about sin because I don't feel sinful. I kept thinking how funny and twisted and strange sex could be, such pantaloons and long skirts hemmed to the ground. I developed a sense of freedom, a young girl riding her favorite horse to make her new born used to the joy of the canter and to wish him to be a boy, besides. Perhaps I saw wifehood coming on. Motherhood, grandmares and I wanted this one last gallop of freedom lost in time or the ability to cope a lifetime in this village."

A rumble of a wagon stopped before them while both seated before the lean-to cottage fully dressed, a young man leaped from the wagon and ran to her, clutching her, crying.

Another rumble from the wagon, the booming voice of a giant man dressed in the Dutch habit.

"Come here, boy. Don't you see she has been whoring with this man?" She with her husband, Janson ran to the feet of another soberly dressed man, her father."

"It's not true, father, it's not true." Curtis was not that much surprised by the melodramatic incident that he could not see some humor.

Marthe hardly tipped him a goodbye as she left with Janson at her side. "I'll prove she has been whoring." He whistled, a dachshund of a larger breed appeared from under a tarpaulin. "Reuben, do what you must do." The dog with alacrity jumped off the wagon, bounced on Curtis in a playful manner and began to smell every inch of his body. When done, he licked Curtis' face, then searched for Marthe who was hiding and he gently began sniffing again, licked her face and returned to the feet of his master. The father took Marthe and his son-in-law into the wagon with announcement.

"Reuben smells nothing. You are innocent. Hitch up!"

Hudson River Valley School

Red Bearded Curtis

CURTIS SALVAGED A LOAF of cheese and some bread, he drank the milk then crossed the cataract. Northward, a rough map of the Valley was in his possession, did not refer to it, avoiding names, descriptions of vacation guides, he chose to see with outdoor sign boards. So he tramped on in a nameless wilderness except for the towns that hugged the river like driven sheep to a safe pasture. This was a day in early November, he ran short of his broth of stiffening paints and turned off at Rennsaeler , at the outskirts, when asking for artist paint he was told there was a quaint curio shop sheeted with beaten copper. A mile or two away, in a village still standing, he saw it soon, a small cottage, a dull copper burnishing in a bright sun. Otherwise, it was a cottage, a stopover for traveling artists of the Hudson Valley School of nigh eighty years ago. A simple carved wood shingle topped a hitching porch which spelled out Schweikert. On the porch stood a rattan chair, an Adirondack chair of cedar, wide slatted that looked uncomfortable.

The sun struggled into the strongly lit interior. A jingling bell announced his presence. An elderly man turned to face him, a clean shaven, kindly face that smiled broadly. He bustled almost falling over an easel.

"Welcome, sir. Welcome to Schweikert. I see you paint. How delightful! Such a long time since, yet occasionally. Have some coffee. Freshly made, my sister Emma Louise brewed it a moment ago. Emma Louise, you wonder, ah! Ah! Named after two aunts, if she had three imagine the result. Possibly Emma Louise Catherine. I tease her all the time."

While the old man gabbled on, unstoppable, he surveyed the premises.

One large room, living quarters above, he imagined. He also imagined it as having been used as a studio, temporary or permanent in the past by a Hudson Valley painter, or the old man himself who could not be a contemporary in years. In taste, everywhere paintings and sketches of all sizes on conventional and weird wood surfaces, remindful of the School or redolent of its subject, the Valley itself.

Bark, flotsam of the river, slabs of oak and white pine, nowhere did he spy a paint tube or can.

"Mr. Schweikert, I came to buy some artist paint. I was told so."

"Why yes, I do have some. I must warn you, it's not the freshest. I did not reorder. We are actually retired, my sister and I, and live with the reminders of Asher and Church and that curious man, Inness."

"You knew them?"

A voice answered from the upstairs. "He's not that old, young man, he knew them in later years when they searched for earlier work when they became famous. He was honored and will tell you about it at insufferable length, if you allow him."

"Emma Louise, I no longer have the breath, you know that."

"I know," she said sassily.

Schweikert remembered with a jolt that painter customer was in the shop to buy paint.

"What colors would you like, sir?"

Emma Louise was now standing beside her brother, look alike except that her hair was still thick, pure white against playful eyes, which caused him to smile.

"Herman, tell the man. Only colors left are some blues, two reds, and while lead. The oil is gone."

Schweikert nodded it was so. However, he did have painting, artifacts of the old School for sale.

"I only have money for paint, Mr. Schweikert. I'll buy what you have."

"All?" the old man said, "I'll be left with no paint. How can I say I own a paint shop anymore?"

"Herman, anymore is never — the paint is crusted. In a year it will be dust. Give it to the young man at no cost and bid him good luck."

"Well said, sister. I was about to do the same." He reached into a drawer and removed twelve cans of paint, handed to him a loving armful. He said "Now we don't expect a masterpiece in the future for our gift, but —"

"I was just about to say Herman, he should give a small token from his backpack to remember him when he becomes famous like the others."

"You read my mind —"

"Mind?"

"Now, Emma Louise —"

"I cannot accept. You are too generous," said Curtis.

"We'll be the judge of that after we have seen what you are going to give us."

"Nothing presentable."

"What a silly word. This a lost world of American native genius."

He shifted from one leg to another, trying to decide whether to forego the paint and not embarrass himself with the painting, or submit and retreat before they hurled it after him. Yesterday, he picked up a clean slab of wild cherry. He cut it six inches by six, and painted it in whites and gray a tiny eddy above which grey birches were naturally pleached to make an arcade of some sort. It was quick brush work, only white lead and black paint left over. He took it out of his bag, looked at it. My God, it was raw looking in the coziness of the cottage, like a piece of meat. He handed it to Herman, but his sister grabbed it and held it to close to her glasses. Herman hurried to her side to view it. They both said nothing, then blurted. "My God, Emma Louise, don't you recognize the eddy by the birches that Inness painted and redid later for a larger canvas?"

"Herman, don't tell me what I see. I see clearly, it is the eddy that Inness painted, and I say, compared to this one of the young man is quite good."

"And why? Anna Maria Louise. Because of a translucence, the freshet is impatient with the slow eddy and solemn birches, hurtling beyond quiet waters to rapids below. To another place which is not our Catskills."

"Come Herman, you are showing off before the young man. Yes, I agree, it is good. Congratulations young man. We feel we have been more than sufficiently repaid for the paint. Now as to Herman's rapturous tendencies, he is referring to the debate among American painters of the school as to intent of painting, sublimity or the beautiful. In our view, and in this I agree with Herman, Inness was a painter not of landscapes alone, but of God and landscape, or could anyone tell them apart. That was Inness' credo. It is yours."

"I don't concern myself with principles of painting or the why. I move my brush."

"That's what Inness said" opined Herman.

"There you go," she said, "imagining things. You were a boy when you met him and he was your age."

"Young man, what is your name, please?"

"Curtis, Anthony."

"I was a dealer for a time. I sold these odds and ends of genius until the fashion was over and faded along with me. I make this offer in the few years left to me and to Anna Marie Louise. To sell your paintings, whatever, if we can. Wherever you go, we know you have no representation. We will keep your work alive and sell to the New York and Los Angeles galleries."

"What have you done with all the rest of your work. Is this all you have? Well?"

"I threw them back into the woods from which they originated."

"But you are wrong! It was a partnership."

"Now Herman, don't get overworked, or esoteric. I know Inness is your favorite, whereas I had a fondness for Church."

"Because he used your grandmother as a model. That's what I call favoritism and not criticism."

Curtis was listening seriously to both, then grinned at the friendly acrimony of brother and sister.

"Don't get yourselves upset. We have a bargain, I agree, why not, you are friendly folk and I trust you, your grey eyes."

"Mine are more green than grey," she said. Curtis stashed the paint into his knapsack. As he rose to leave, they clung to him, begging him to stay for the day. "Anna Marie Louise would bake and cook a fresh turkey. And —"

Impulsively he kissed them both and left. From a short distance he saw them in the doorway. He saw tears glistening like frozen rain.

The Quarry

ON THE APPALACHIAN TRAIL he walked about 100 miles, and stopped to rest two days at a hiker's shelter. Signs to Concord, not far off, from Walden Pond, David Thoreau's hut on the river. A thought! Why doesn't he build a hut on the river, to live in solitude and stillness, and paint, as Thoreau wrote of nature's wonders. Curtis did not think so, there was an imperative at his feet that drove him through mountain valleys, and ridges, more like a dancer. He tipped his brush in salutation to the hermit of New England. Curtis was driven by a lyricism of his brush, he thought at that moment.

Still in the valley days later at Saugerties on the junction to a road to the right that led fifty miles to West Rutland. On the corner a surveyor asked him to renew an old sign, which he did. He was repaid enough to buy a lumber jacket, a hood, and a pair of woolen gloves. While speaking to the storekeeper he mentioned looking for a direct route to the White Mountains, the clerk asked the Green Mountains, or the White Mountains?

"Why? Is there a difference? Not all the same?"

The clerk rounded the counter to claim proudly that the White Mountain was better to see, for it was really white, a pearly white. As a sight-seer he would surely prefer it to the greenness of the Green Mountain Range. The clerk enjoyed his perplexity and explained. "The mountain I am referring to is in West Rutland quarry. Half a mountain, sliced in half by saws and hammers of the marble workers, exposing the

inner surface which was the source of the most popular monumental construction in the country, Vermont marble."

"It would take me out of my way. I am going North."

"Wherever you are going, you will never see again the innards of a mountain. You are a painter, I see the edge of a canvas."

"Yes, I suppose."

"Then don't miss it. Right from here and straight on. You should reach the quarry by dusk. Hang on until morning and treat yourself. Only two inns along the way and the temperature is falling." He pointed to a huge thermometer over an iron safe. "I used to work at the quarry before my eyes failed me but the sight of that quarried mountain would revive my sight. Maybe I gazed at it too long, its luminosity blinded me. Perhaps," he said coming closer, "you will paint it for me so I can view it without damage to my eyes."

"You respect me too much."

"Whatever, a remembrance is good even if not equal to the original."

"You promise?"

"Yes."

"Take this half dollar for a hearty lunch. If you come back this way, drop by. I'd appreciate even a daubing."

"I'll take your address and if a painting happens, I shall send it to you."

"A compass in my brain. That's all I can say."

"Veer west to the quarry. It may be your destination after all."

"Why do you say destination?"

"You seem to be guided."

"That's fanciful."

"Not in the country of ministers."

He winced at the word ministers. He did not belong. He was a pariah to a minister!

"Mountains are a specialty in these parts, don't you know?" The clerk gabbled on.

He thanked the purblind clerk, made a right turn as he left the shop

causing the clerk to smile with satisfaction. It was after dusk when he reached the quarry limits identified by broken plinths. Scrap marble and rubble. He sloshed all forty miles by hitching on backs of wagons. He knew he was flanked by rising heights because they filled the night with their own darkness, ahead a newly up-graded road and a cluster of yellow lights from lanterns. He passed cottages closing shutters, lights dimming, time for sleep for these early risers. But as darkness overcame him, there was a distant glow ahead. When he came closer he saw a hut brightly lit, through paned glass he saw two men seated at a table playing cards. One man was tending a huge Franklin stove, another shorter, tending copper coffee pots or "machinette" on top of the red hot stove. He saw no women, assumed it was a coffee house or a club house where the men gathered for a drink or a game of cards after supper.

It was so.

He opened the door and was greeted with astonishment. One asked the other who is he. All shook heads but they were smiling at him generously.

The coffee tender, who was the owner asked him to sit down, pulling up a chair, signaling that he should remove his wet outerwear, which he did.

"Signore, you are welcome. Why you come? You have coffee, very strong, forte."

"Yes, thank you."

"Maybe some grappa from the old country?"

"Grazie."

"Ah, you speaka Italian?"

"No, just a phrase."

"Bene. Your name?"

"Anthony Curtis."

"Thissa here is Arnaldo. Michele, and Fosco. I am Nicolo. We all from Toscana, in Italy. Fourteen families all come to do marble many years ago."

Curtis animated by the warmth and the geniality of his host lifted his tumbler of grappa and said, "Salute."

"Bravo," said Nicolo at the table. "He makes nice with the speech."

Arnaldo was first annoyed at the interruption of a good hand as briscola, joined in. "What you here for?"

"I come to see the quarry."

Arnaldo turned to Fosco, "Che cose dici?"

"La montagna bianca."

He noted some confusion, Curtis described the reputed side of a mountain."

"Ho capito," said Nicolo, "you marble worker?"

"No, I consider myself a painter."

"Ma bravo! Bravo! Sei un compagno d'arte."

"A modest painter," said Curtis modestly.

"Guardi, che modesta, che dici tutti quanti, e il nostro fratello, si o no?"

"Ma si!" was the concerted reply.

Nicolo looked at the window. "Fa notte, e scuro. Ora di chiudere."

"E questo signore. Dove dorme?"

"Si spiega, la mattina in via a lavorelo portiamo a vedere la sua montagna bianca."

"Bravo Nicolo, sei un uomo do compassione per il nostro nuovo fratello."

Nicolo explained to Curtis who already half understood. "You brother, you sleep here. In morning, we show you montagna. You be careful no make fire, you take care of fire. Keep coal hot for morning coffee. You understand, Capisce?"

"Si!"

"E bravo," joked Arnaldo. "Incomincia a toscaneggiare."

In cypress blue darkness, he was awakened by the foursome "fratelli" and a large man who towered above them, a head taller than Curtis.

Arnaldo spoke, "Me, show you another fratello. Signore Oreste Fioravant, your new 'fratello,' he big foreman."

They first climbed a steep hill which leveled under crushed stone. Ahead a tunneled darkness as the overtopping firs blocked any light from a lightening sky and the sides were flanked by mounds of discarded marble mined over fifty years.

He was at Oreste's side when it happened. He fell to the ground when he saw the concaved mountain ahead of him. It loomed like a luminescent planet. The dawn light played on it. First a crimson, then green, then pearly white, then a whiteness that was unimaginable in paint or even in Nature as he saw it. He was struggling with words, he wanted to shout God Almighty! Oreste thought he had a fit, placed his gnarled finger under his tongue suspecting epilepsy, Curtis shoved it away.

Oreste gave Curtis air and picked him up. Curtis was dazed. Oreste said softly, "We are used to it, Mr. Curtis. I should have warned you, but could I say that I could describe it."

Curtis shaded his eyes and looked again, more beautiful with detail, a royal purple along the edge. It seemed as this marble were the color template of all marbles. He was steady, he assured Oreste, who still held him. Oreste said "To react so, Mr. Curtis, you must be an artist!"

Curtis stumbled, his eyes still on the wonderment before him.

He always believed mountains in situ to be beautiful, but never the interior. He thought of the interior as a flaming fumurole of ashes and pumice. As he came closer and the dawn light receded, the stone marble face turned a sort of dirty gray which disappointed him. Oreste knew what was on his mind and smiled indulgently, "Light makes the marble live."

"I seem to have nothing to live for but this North."

Pierina

"NORTH? WHAT IS THIS North?" huffed Pierina, fluffing her red peasant skirt in amazement.

Curtis having dinner with the foreman, Oreste, in his sturdy cottage in a village of cottages, large, and small at the foothills of the quarry.

The street was paved with slabs of quarry that ran the length of the village, of chalet-like lodgings. There was at the end a square, in the center of roughly carved marble. In the rear of the cottages were vegetable gardens, grapevines, and fruit trees. Also signs of cooperage oak barrels and strips of binding twine. From the cottage were suspended clotheslines hemming space. The rooftops of cedar shingles were whitened by marble dust that scoured from the shadowing quarry.

It was a settlement of Carrara marble artisans from Tuscany. Forty years ago, there were 220 artisans. Oreste Fioravanti was a huge foreman, and Mayor. Oreste was a stocky man with large shoulders, a kindly splat nosed face, clean shaven, unlike his "brothers", Arnaldo and the rest. His voice was baritonal from a deep chest.

"Pierina! behave per carita."

Her first words on greeting Curtis were "Where are you going?" with unwanted petulance.

Curtis' reply was a terse, "North".

Pierina, 22 years old, of soubrette height, slim waisted in her blue blouse, large, almost myopic eyes, pretty nose slightly aquiline, and strong teeth between moist lips. Her hair was tressed, and deep blonde.

She was indignant without a cause, so thought Curtis.

"Papa, what is North?"

"Maybe Canada, adesso basta!"

"Canada! They speak French! You speak the French?"

"Not really."

"Then why you go up North?"

"I don't know." Curtis wondered at this reply. He did not know the answer which often perplexed him.

"You silly man." said Pierina preparing the machinetta of black coffee. "You a salesman?"

Oreste expostulated loudly, "Pierina, Mr. Curtis is not a traveling salesman. He is a painter, an artist looking for subjects."

"Then why doesn't he love marble like you do, and stay?"

"Pierina, you are my only daughter, the image of your sainted mother, don't shame me before my guest, Mr. Curtis."

Pierina took a deep breath, "Papa, I am sorry. I apolgize Signor Curtis." She rose quickly, blushing at her father's scolding, kicked up her heels, her shoes were painted, and retreated to the kitchen.

"That's where I belong, in the kitchen, Papa."

Oreste poured more wine for his guest. Pierina's importunate questioning of the handsome red bearded young man was understood by him. It was part of a sad story of courtship.

Before Oreste attempted to explain, Pierina was back with an excuse of more coffee, and sat now quietly and demurely, obedient.

Oreste began to tell Curtis of the amenities of Rutland, USA, the lovely milky countryside, the easy access of the finest marble, a community for all artists among stone artisans, and the subjects for his easel, the Green Mountains, the sunrise plane of the quarry. Oreste swilled ruefully, he was playing Pierina's game. Here, was a site for a husband! Like daughter, like father. Like Pierina he liked Curtis. First hand he saw talent, and a good person. A man who fell to his knees before the beauty of raw marble, could not be bad, or a bad husband for his dear Pierina, who had been unlucky in love. Betrothed twice –

Curtis listened to the enticements, sipping a strong dago red. What made Pierina think he did not like Rutland, or the village. He felt at home, among friends –

Pierina stood up, lips pursed, thoughtful, her breast subdued. She kissed her father goodnight, and tapped Curtis' hand, and she left for her room.

The dinner was rich with polenta and sausage and a fried vegetable platter, and fruit.

Oreste and Curtis stayed up late smoking cigars.

"A traveling painter with no roots, no clients. How will you live?"

"I need little."

"A studio, a home?"

Curtis stood up to curtail the conversation. Oreste signaled that he sit down and listen."

"Then you don't care much about your life, your future."

"I refuse to think in that mode."

"Then think this, you marry Pierina."

"Your daughter, Pierina?"

"Yes, mia figlia!"

"Signore Fioravanti, is this wine too robusto for you?"

"My feelings for Pierina are, it is an outrageous and daring proposition. I'll explain, in one year was engaged two times to worthy men. The two fidanzati died. One from a fall and the other one crushed under a machine. They were paesano of my choice of good families."

Curtis slugged more wine to remain courteous to his host.

"Died in the quarry, now Tuscana are superstitious and believe the same things. The families of sons now believe that a spell has been placed on Pierina and any man who becomes engaged to her will die violently in the quarry as poor Pierina was a witch of doom for young suitors. So now Pierina, my poor child will never marry. She is a very ardent young woman. She will never marry under this alleged curse."

"But what has poor Pierina's misfortune got to do with me?"

"Nothing at all — unless you agree?"

"Agree! What did you put in this dago red?"

"A father's love for his only daughter."

"Who can doubt it?"

"Now listen Signore Curtis to what I say, on her behalf, and you may profit too."

"Right now, I'll profit by more of your excellent wine."

"You must keep your senses. Hear me out. You stay awhile here, not as my guest. I find nice room for you with friends, no plot, see?"

"I see."

"Pierina likes you. She did not cry too much when they died, she was disappointed. With us, marriages are arranged but with you it's different. She likes you very much. I don't say she is hard-hearted. She thought they were spiteful to deny her a marriage bed. I speak frankly. She is still much of a child."

"I get you a job here in quarry as painter, sculptor, you stay one month. You court Pierina two weeks, you become fidanzato two weeks then you go away. All paesani say Pierina has a fidanzato and nothing happen."

Curtis laughed sputtering wine.

"How do you know the curse will not be fatal for me?"

"Because, I don't believe in it. The men were careless. They are not getting compensation, that is proof."

"Maybe."

"All day spell broken good Pierina get betrothed, nothing happen to fidanzato. Meanwhile a marble pergola was ordered from the Drayfield quarry, which you admire so much. You will make the first design and we will copy it in marble. Imagine working with Vermont marble. Signore Curtis, Michelangelo would envy you."

"Then wedding bells, no. No, much as I like you Mr. Curtis, I would prefer a paesan for Pierina. You are too sophisticated."

"Grazie," Curtis said with some added sarcasm.

"Senti, after you do the pergola, you leave. You don't come back. Pierina cry, I cry, the paesani cry but now the suitors come on for her hand. You see the curse is broken in their minds!"

"You work by yourself in the old museum. We bring you the best marble that will make you cry and bow in veneration. Simple,but highly decorated. An artist with knowledge of flowers and vines, as you have shown in your samples."

It is not Pierina that was irresistible to Curtis, it was the marble pergola.

"I know you will not dishonor the marble. Don't dishonor my daughter."

"That is a wry thought, father Oreste."

"Senza poesia."

"I should say."

In the coming weeks, the banns were announced by the priest and Pierina was happy as a lark, the delectable one. He was ecstatic working furiously with a clay model of the pergola which the finishers and polishers watched with admiration. He hated to waste the powdered marble, if he had bread he would be tempted to eat it whole-somely. Used to viewing mountains bare or bare from an angle or topside, he was working within the life of the stone that seemed to be alive under his hands.

He felt an uncanny guidance in all he did. The flowers, rose, gentian verbena, globules of purple grape inherent in the marble. All the paesani gathered up to watch the progress and exclaimed 'che meraviglia!' And of course, Pierina was proud as punch, thus was her husband's future. 'Che fortuna' for Pierina. The day arrived, the pergola finished. Curtis appeared with a dowry of five hundred dollar bills from Oreste and brush kissed her, and left the village.

When weeks went by and no word from Curtis, yes, later, he was married and Pierina whimpered again and put away her third wedding dress. But as suitors appeared for her hand now that the spell was broken, she complained that Signore Anthony was a mandolin with one string that played one tune, 'North, North!'

Treasure of the Himalayas

BEFORE CURTIS LEFT, ASKED Oreste for a way directly North, not on routes but on a biker's path, across the valleys and peaks. Oreste led him to a cutaway trail used by tree farmers of years ago. It was overgrown and along the way Curtis was forced to remove fallen branches, and limbs. Dimly lit, heavily pined, he sought slats of light to paint. He traveled in this manner for four days in dropping temperatures. He had provided himself with a collapsible tent and a woolen blanket. He had to warm his tubes in his palms. Still, he painted with a stiffened brush, the internal darkness of the forest, and its palpable silence. Finally on the fifth day, he stood on a steep ridge of a valley overlooking a sodden clearing at the bottom, cleared of boulders. It appeared unnatural to him. As he descended, he saw the outline of an airfield, hangers, and there airplanes. He saw blinking lights, and soon heard the purr of airplane engines. On the planes he saw no markings of a base which consisted of three hangers, a large building, and a garage. He was close now, the purr was a roar of turning engines. He sat down to paint the scene when a jeep pulled up with a screech, two soldiers leaped from the cab, seized him without a word, and tumbled him into the rear, painting gear and all.

Curtis yelled, "What are you doing?"

A soldier answered gruffly, "lucky we didn't shoot you on sight."

The jeep raced into the compound and stopped at an administrative building. Curtis was escorted with belongings to an office, and handcuffed to a chair. The door opened, a brisk officer entered, stood before Curtis, starring at him curiously.

A soldier spoke: "we saw him on the hill, spying on the base."

"Spying?"

"Even got a paint box."

"Is that so? You are a painter, and a spy."

"I am a painter, sir. Anthony Curtis. I look for subjects."

"Such as a secret airbase? Curtis don't be innocent. We are the law and judges here."

"I don't know what you are talking about. I stumbled on this base."

"Miles from nowhere! You will be detained and questioned and shot if proven guilty of spying." To the soldiers, "look him up."

Turning to Curtis, "you say you are a painter?"

"Yes, sir."

"While we investigate you, you can be helpful, it may help your cause. Can you paint a fuselage of a plane?"

"Anything," said Curtis.

"Very well, we'll see. Lock him up."

Curtis was locked into a make-shift jail with his belongings after being searched. He was fed and bedded on an army cot. There he speculated for three days trying to understand his predicament. Why the security? Why the secret base? Why was he a spy? His shoes were still powdered with marble dust.

On the fourth day, a soldier appeared with no stripes, no one wore any noncom stripes or insignia, neither the officers.

The soldier wore fatigues, spotted with paint.

"I am told you are a painter."

"I am."

"We came to get you. We are short handed. Can you paint a fuselage?"

"I think so."

"Well, come with me until the commandant is ready for you."

Curtis was given fatigues and led to a hanger which contained a high speed plane uncamouflaged. He was given a paint can, and a wide brush and told to paint the long fuselage. After three days of painting, he asked to see the commandant. He had something important to say. A confession, some thought.

When he arrived at headquarters, the commandant sidled away while introducing him to a man who looked like a President, in a grey suit.

"Curtis, you have a confession, this is Mr. Wilkins, of the CIA."

"I am Anthony Curtis." Mr. Wilkins, a tall man, well dressed, in his fifties with a narrow face and undershot teeth said, "I am Sam Wilkins. I am here to hear what you have to say. Who hired you?"

"Sir, I am an independent painter. I came to complain about your paint."

"Our paint?" Wilkins smiled. "It's not for your easel."

"Your fuselage."

"Good."

"I have been painting the surfaces for three days, when in the sun I noticed a grittiness that flaked under my brush. I think the paint you are using is defective and will flake off in flight. That is my opinion."

"Well, that is news. Then no confession?"

"A complaint."

"Actually, you are an artist painter of some repute."

"That is news, sir."

"However, we must make precautions."

"I shall ask that the paint be tested in a wind tunnel. You will hear from me."

"I must take you seriously, camouflaging is a kind of art, and you are an artist."

True to his word, the painted fuselage was tested in the wind tunnel.

A pilot was ordered to occupy the cockpit and the wind tunnels were revved to combat velocity in dives and cold altitudes. Nothing could be seen from the ground. But when the pilot exited, he told the major the windshield became so pockmocked that he could barely see ahead.

Mr. Wilkins — CIA

CURTIS WAS SUMMONED TO see Mr. Wilkins.

"Mr. Curtis, you are not a spy, nor sabateur."

"No, sir."

"You traveled a lonely life, painting mountains. I too am a mountain specialist, after a fashion. I am not asking you to remain here under duress as a workman. What are your plans?"

"Heading North."

"According to my report, that is always your reply."

"Mr. Wilkins, I follow the mountains."

"Not so strange, I do too, you may still. Certain matters are under study that my require your active assistance."

"I can't imagine."

"We'll see. In the meantime, be comfortable. I have requisitioned suitable clothes for you and money until we decide how we can use your valuable talent."

North

Two days later, Sam Wilkins, CIA, sent for him again.

"First let me express the thanks of the Air Force for the discovery of the defect of the paint. The Mgs are enough to handle without handicapping ourselves. So thanks. You will receive an award for your discovery. So let's get on, Curtis. We know something about you. The FBI has cased you, an excellent family, both families with military records, parents unknown but known to us, excellent American stock, lazy student at Columbia, gentlemen's Cs. Dabbled in painting on Morningside Heights, the nearby park when you should be in classes. Got mixed up with Beatniks for a year, believed them, got soulful with them, and so on — fed up with kinky sex, got fed up. Suffered a breakdown at Bellevue for six months, deep depression, nothing organic, they said it was a religious crisis and you disappeared. Next time we track you, you are in the Hudson Valley, Adirondacks painting mountains and streams. You did meritorious sculpture of a pergola, an exhibition in Chicago, and those Italians in West Rutland love you.

He stood before Curtis stiffly. "What I am about to tell you Curtis is utterly confidential and of the highest order if I have a mission for you. I'll explain, but we must have the word of honor of the member of the Curtis family that if you refuse, your mouth will be shut forever. Of course, you cannot answer now. You know nothing at this point, so here goes — you don't have to listen, you can walk out."

Curtis sat down.

"We are manning a mission to far Asia, to the Himalayas to be exact. And that fact may be of interest to you as a painter of mountain ranges. Aerial reconnaissance of the range has proved fruitless because of the high velocity winds, incessant storming and false configuration of snow. Camera film goes grey in that area, the Tibetans have some of the fine mountains where their superstition originates. We need a painter. Naturally, we have hearsay knowledge, guesses of explorers, the actual depth of valleys, some military features hidden on mountains side, emplacements. We know patrols of China have routes, bandits have hideaways, that is all of interest to us. Even India, an ally has interest in its topography. Needless to say, this is a secret mission unknown to anyone not in this room or part of the crew and experts. From a military point of view I know this scan of the Himalayas is of no interest to you. It is the natural beauty of the range which might invite you in the mission.

Curtis replied. "That is so. I'll paint and you may enjoy it or see some advantages. I must tell you frankly from what I have studied and seen. I think the range is impenetrable to you, however I'll go along just to take a view of that wonder."

"Well. The CIA wishes to index the entire world and the range is missing on its index cards. You will have experts with you, a geologist from Russian Georgi. A gemologist and interpreter of the local languages who is half native of some tribe."

"A curious combo for a military expedition. Why the gemologist?"

"As you know the Ural mountains in Russia have provided Russia with much of its wealth in emeralds, rubies, diamonds and the like. There are mining companies here who are itching to find out if the Himalayas are similarly rich in gems. We are too, the CIA. There are rumor of troves of gems hidden in the mountains mined centuries ago, the first Aryans."

"One condition, I can paint whatever I like?"

"Yes, you see we have no guidance. It is serendipity and an artist in our opinion may be lucky where experts miss out. The CIA is always innovative."

"I'll need a plentiful supply of paint, brushes, canvasses and a native to carry it along. I'll need three pair of sunglasses shaded in tints."

"Anything, else?"

"I hope to produce works of art whether or not they will ever see civilization again."

"I agree and you see the risk of their destruction in the event of capture or worse —"

"What does the CIA desire most?"

"The world perhaps?"

"The Himalayas have already conquered the Heavens!"

"Interesting — the heavens you say."

"I am ready."

"You came from a patriotic tradition. I shall be curious to see your paintings. By the way, I never asked you if you agreed to this mission."

"I do – when the subject is mountains."

The droning of the high powered plane was incessant when Wilkins resumed.

"Curtis you are headed for a secret airfield at the foothills of the Himalayas. The flight will take several days with refueling stopovers. You will lack nothing. Your gear is stowed away. After all, you need only a paint brush. In a way, you are our man on this flight really, of the painting? A self-indulgence or a rapture or discovery? Only the product could be a judge."

He supervised the repainting of the secret planes fuselage with approved paint and tested in a wind tunnel, a pilot beside him.

Finally the day arrived for his departure to the Himalayas, 600 million years younger. The result of the traveling and painting was in his knapsack, two paintings on oak panels, the rest he gave away or strewn along the way. He could not be burdened with the panels and canvasses. What was the purpose?

Near Canada, not far from Lake Champlain, he said to himself that he was headed for a younger breed, of mountains.

The Jungle Camp

The so called landing was so tentative, only huge tents sheltered three mechanics, two pilots, a hundred or so Sherpa porters, Indians and the passengers, separately.

A lingering jungle surrounded the camp, ringed by groves of giant rhododendrons, azaleas and vine suffocated trees.

Hordes of butterflies, glistening giant dragonflies and fewer flying insects. The sun was warm, the air not tepid, and the nights cold. At the foothills of the chosen mountain, Curtis could not see the peak cloaked in heavy mist rising from the snow cover. The camp was an upland slope. A climbing trail used by butter-faced Buddist pilgrims to the lower reaches of the mountain where there were rock-hewn temples to worship. The holy mountain marked on a map held by the Georgian in full regalia of dress, day and night. No predators at night, the Sherpas were famished and so was the British interpreter who gobbled her ration. According to the gemologist, the camp was on the site of an ancient river bed of a glacial river that once coursed down the mountain. The gemologist shouted a source of emeralds.

No water buffalo, strange stiles, tall stalks of bamboo, and tall orchids. Curtis wondered, could that be the aim of the so-called military mission according to Mr. Wilkins, emeralds? The gemologist grunted happily, and played with his pocket pebbles. Curtis sketched a blue and golden butterfly as large as a bird. It lay still for him to sketch, he was impatient to add a color, when it lofted away. It was sacred to the Sherpas who fed it honey. The air was perfumed by the preponderance of blooming varieties of small and giant azaleas, rhododendrons rose everywhere with profusions of saucer-sized flowers heavily scented about which teemed vari-colored birds and parrots.

Dewed vapors of hillside, wild flowers greeted the morning.

The Georgian was in command although this was according to Mr. Wilkins, a USA enterprise. He growled, fingered his dagger, kicked the ground, he was impatient, he was in the vicinity before, he needed no guide or advice.

He scorned Curtis, thought him useless baggage, and could not understand his presence, so he ignored him. There was a delay in the climb up the mountain, a rock fall on the trail blocked any movement. Curtis painted the bluebells on the sides of a near valley. In the shadow of the mountain, Curtis saw no sunrise, no sunsets, only their fiery glow that suffused the sky. It was galling. He could not duplicate or suggest, it required gigantic brush strokes.

To Curtis' surprise, the phantom rose overhead and left with the two pilots. His companions too were surprised but they had confidence in the promise of Mr. Wilkins, unknown to Curtis. As a precaution Curtis checked his issued rifle and ammunition, and a package of rations. At last, they were packed, the mules in line, Sherpas gestured as porters to trek to the pilgrim trail led by the joyful Georgian, followed by the interpreter and gemologist and Curtis lagging behind laden with easel and paint box. Upland, to the mountain, suddenly, the trail was paved cleanly.

Vultures Feast

DAYS EARLIER, IN THEIR seats he met his companions on the mission, a huge Georgian who hardly spoke, a body guard, and a mining engineer who had been on a Russian expedition some years before. He was wrapped in gold bracelets, neckband, rings, even the hilt of a scabbard dagger at his side of his immense bulk. Also a German born gemologist with small stones in his pockets, not gems. He was short, stocky, an expert in Swastika lore. The interpreter was an unusually tall British woman in her role in the mission, the height of Curtis over six feet, large breasts, a tube-like waist and long spindly legs like high calipers that the short geologist might use. She spoke three languages and only spoke when spoken to.

Now briefed intensely. If they were captured would the enemy make of them, whoever they turned out to be. Chinese patrols, desert bandits, perhaps gold miners, miners of emeralds. It had an oily tongue. But hurrah! He would see the Himalayas. What was the image of silky wiliness never explained by Mr. Wilkins. But North of everything. Worth his life? And what did his seatside companion gamble? The gemologist? The Georgian riches? The interpreter? What? payoff? when the four passengers boarded days ago.

The plane had risen to a great height over the ocean, and island stopovers. Curtis cleaned his brushes, catching up with his memory, as if were writing an obituary. The desolation of the Beatniks, his church and foster parents, their goodness, his adolescent antics with the Beats, the kindness of Oreste and Pierina, his vague guilt of jilting her, the gentle homage to painting, the hokey spiritualism of the Beats. Susan would say "Her dear boys." Obituary? Did he sense a real personal danger in the mission? His companions did not seem fearful. The Georgian slept clutching his dagger, twitching. The gemologist counted his countless pebbles and the interpreter ate constantly with helpings of curry. The phantom landed.

He saw a once healthy resort at the foothills of the Himalaya, lengthened to accommodate Phantom runs. Upon landing six half bred sherpas were assigned to them as carrier and escort armed with Mauser rifles, and were soon billeted a half mile on an uphill trail.

Behind giant azalea, rhododendron and fir trees Curtis saw the rising rim of a mountain. At last, he could almost bow to the coming wonders to behold as the pilgrims did. Affording a magnificent miniature view of the range to come, Curtis thought they were huge monstrances of a long lasting religion of the Vedas he remembered from his Beatnik days. The Georgian plowed in his high boots ahead of the leading sherpas, while the spindly interpreter kept pace with the vanguard of the sherpas. Curtis stayed in between, stopping so often to make a sketch, impossible to paint, since the Georgian kept up this hurried pace.

When they came to a rest, Curtis was struck intoxicated by the accompanying view which was the sides of the massive stone effigy.

The Treasure

THE NEXT DAY WAS a trek. Curtis was on the paved slabs easing the climb which rose steeper with every step.

He now saw the peak and into canyons, and valleys, connecting like iridescent serpents. He stopped to paint. It happened all too soon, the Georgian slapped his sides, his memory was correct. He stopped before a high bluff and asked Curtis to survey with his painter's eyes the wall behind the edge of the bluff. Curtis saw nothing worthwhile and refused; the Georgian's knife was at his throat. "You do what I say, I tell Mr. Wilkins."

Curtis gazed up at the bluff that was covered thickly with vines creating a sort of rustic balcony. He saw nothing unusual or what he was supposed to look for but something caught his eye, a scroll on the wall.

"It's a scroll," called Curtis behind the bluff against the wall. It may not be but it does not look like a cranny or a nest."

The Georgian was first on the bluff by a roundabout path. The puffing German next, Curtis was carrying a pad and crayon. The interpreter stayed below. She skinned her knees on the first ascent. She waited silently. While the Georgian howled with the pleasure of discovery, he wiped away the grime from the scroll. It was a hardly decipherable Swastika, a symbol of ancient Aryans who since populated the region. The Georgian eagerly pick axed the scroll into fragments and began digging effectively into a stoppage of a hole about six feet in diameter that appeared to be an opening. The pick broke through, tumbling rubble and earth upon their feet. All were struck by a rainbow ray of hues as the sun struck the opening of the cavern. Eyes dazzled, finally focused they saw on a stone slab a huge mound of precious gems, emeralds, diamonds and rubies, of size and grandeur never seen before on earth so thought Curtis, and especially the German, who began to cry with overwhelming joy. In the echoing banks of the mountains, each sound became exaggerated.

As the Georgian reached with his prepared leather bags for loot, they heard a scream. Curtis looked down, a scruffy bandit held the head of the interpreter on his rusty bayonet, still screaming. He turned away his eyes only to see another bandit split the Georgian in two with slices of his bayonet while another cut the throat of the surprised German. A rope had been slung over the side of the bluff to helo the interpreter earlier. Curtis grabbed it. It was too short to reach the ground or allow him to jump without breaking a limb and was helpless for a bayonet or worse so he clung to the rope while the bandits now all gather on the bluff to share the loot of gems, laughing toothlessly, letting him hang until they had time to kill him. The bluff was short and not deep. Enough room for the burly bandits to move the gems. One end of the rope was tied to an old root. Curtis decided that he could not hang on much longer. He decided to swing the rope by leveraging against the wall of the bluff, swing aside and maybe catch the bandit's feet under the rope and tripping them over the bluff. He leveraged both feet as hard as he could and swung, the rope caught the feet of the bandit and toppled all three into a small gorge where they lay still. Curtis climbed the rope to the bluff, the Georgian was dead, flies all over him. The gemologist was on his side, his eyes gouged by crows, he looked down, the interpreter was bone white among a swarm of vultures.

Curtis shoved the Georgian and the German into the gorge with the bandits. He could not stand the sight and there was nothing to be done. The gems were still in the hole only disturbed by the greedy fingers of the Georgian, seemingly intact as a whole trove. The bluff was slimed with blood. He threw earth upon it to gain a footing, to rest while he planned what to do with the trove, the Himalayas heart of gems, the object of Mr. Wilkins' CIA mission. The noble Aryan tribe who venerated the Himalaya evidently did not rape the mountains of the gems but preserved a dedication to the God of the mountain.

It was not to be used for evil and never will as Curtis decided to plug up the treasure hole and prevent its use for evil or commerce. Before he plugged it completely, he did take two rubies and a large diamond for himself. He was broke, abandoned in a dangerous country with uncertain friends. What about Wilkins? He would suspect with the loss of his accomplice the Georgian and the German, the interpreter, that Curtis has the loot. His CIA would be after him all over the world for such a treasure, Mr. Wilkins and CIA. He pocketed the gems, sealed the hole as best he could, rooted it with vine sprouts and ascended the upper level of the hillside. Luckily he saw loose rocks above the bluff. He found a stave and leveraged the boulders into the bluffs surface covering it with solid stone. The bodies in the gorge would disappear overnight as vultures had time to crack the bones and leave no trace of a human body.

Abandoned

CURTIS NEVER HAD LETTERS of introduction anywhere. His passport was North and he was quite North on this hemisphere. He got by, but Tibet from what he saw, was another case. As he ambled along, he saw one more piteous case of want, suffering and crippling diseases than he would ever wish to see again in any lifetime. One wrenched his heart. A girl perhaps sixteen but shrunken by paralysis lay in a small dogcart which apparently was her place in this universe. Two huge mastiffs lay between the two shafts, lean as scrap leather. An old woman sat by, in front of a small hut which was their home. As he approached the cart of willow or rattan, the hounds did not growl or move, so Curtis leaned to give the girl some paper money. Although undergrown by her illness, her mind acted older and she thanked him with a sprightly smile which surprisingly was toothful and white. The mother stood up, lithe for an old lady, she had been a palace dancer.

Tibet, the outskirts Curtis could not predict the filth, the squalor, the running disease, the stench of excrement and urine, the mangy dogs, huddled rags out of which peeped grimed and toothless faces. Huts and cairn holds out of which spumed revolting aromas. Wherever the ground rose with a view of the Himalaya peak, there stood a domino like done of immaculate whiteness. But the contrast was greater when more snow covered peaks reared into view to subject Tibet to groveling abjection.

Faces grinned friendly-like but those were the faces of thieves, ingratiating themselves to a stranger. Others were too miserable to respond to any novelty at all.

Curtis returned to an abandoned airfield, the buildings already vandalized, and little remaining, the Phantoms were gone, pilots, and mechanics, and native workers. It had reverted to the jungle plain. He found an empty paint can in which he secreted three gems. Now he must find his further way to the American Consul, if one existed.

The Lamasery

HE SLINKED ALONG THE darkening road, alert for the presence of bandits, clinging to the roadside growth of giant azaleas. No one was in sight on the downward slope to the camp. He hoped he might hear the roar of the Phantom engines. Then ahead, he saw a building with a wrecked pagoda of weathered wood. A door was ajar, windows shattered, and beams askew. As he approached warily, he noted religious inscriptions on the lintel and a loosely hanging bell soundless in glacial wind. No sign of any life. He hurried, night was falling fast. He was lost. He needed shelter of any kind. He reached the building and realized close up, that it was a looted lamasery. The door creaked and fell in his arms. He restored it and entered the ruined lamasery to find one large room. The earthen floor was littered with shards of pottery, and rusting tin utensils. About the walls still hanging were shredded flags and molded tapestries desecrated by the bandits and desperados. In the dimming light, he saw in a far corner what appeared to be an altar of polished stone. He gathered some grass and leaves and covered the slab relic and lied down. His legs were bruised on the swing down. Curtis didn't need his eyes, he was surrounded by darkness. He drew several worn tapestries from the rubble with which to cover himself against the cold. Tapestries of painted demons and devils who would protect him situated on their altar. The lone bell under the force of the increasing wind began to sound weakly. Curtis thought maybe irony is the forefather of death. He did not expect to survive the cold. But his eyes closed, and he fell asleep as the bell tolled weakly. What awakened him at dawn was the cawing of large crows, the size of ravens, standing about him. His eyes still in his head, the crows had no time to peck them. They were foraging for food, spying him they imagined the llamas were back and eating food. He kicked at them, they barely moved making sure that he was really alive. Finally the crows flew off with well-disappointed cawing. Curtis threw off his covers and sat up. Immediately, he felt the change in the weather, no snow, and the altar was warmer. He walked to the door, the bell ceased jangling in a mild breeze, no mist. He did not realize in a cold torpor he had slept for two days.

Curtis fell against a tumulus of termites which supported his back, he found a painter's rag in his pocket to staunch the blood from a wound on his brow. Every breath was painful by constriction. Not a thought in his brain, all that happened was all reflex, the assault by the bandits, his going North, only a mindless, murderous reflex to a violent death? Gone is his paint box, his brushes, his sketches. Without them he had no purpose, no North. Was he just a Sam Wilkins, CIA deviant? His painting ploy was a lure to a treasure! He could still hear the gnawing of bones, then all was quiet. He tried to rise, fell back. He lay back, and waited for more strength. Yes, he escaped an attempt on his life. Why was he spared? Spared? When the sun rose, he would be found crawling with termites.

When he was executed, he would be fed to the greedy eyed revolting carrion of the grey vultures.

Pierina asked, "What is marble?" in her petulant accent.

Oreste said, "Light is the life of marble."

So? He could see the peak of it tinged by the rising sun.

No movement. Breathing better, not in gulps, steadily the pain of his body was easing, soon he would be able to stand, and walk to the French hospital.

Hours later, when he was upright, he was surrounded by the Chamberlain's guards.

They tied his hands behind his back, and waited with bayonets fixed. He gripped his paint can.

The Arrest

SOMEONE TAPPED HIM LIGHTLY on the shoulder. It was the Chamberlain accompanied by a guard of six soldiers. The guards shoved the girl and the cart nearby aside, the mastiffs growling in protest. The Chamberlain raised the hem of his magnificent robes from the underlying filth.

"Welcome to Tibet, Mr. Curtis. Mr. Wilkins was concerned about you. At last, we found you."

"Mr. Wilkins inquired?" said Curtis suspiciously.

"Yes, you are an American citizen under our protection, and his."

"Thank you. I can manage on my own."

"I doubt it, Mr. Curtis. You are under arrest on the testimony of a Chinese bandit. Look at yourself, you are in virtual rags, torn, bloodied, a sight, I must say."

"Arrest is an ugly word, Mr. Curtis, but you will accompany me to the palace of the Princess where you will be attended to and treated for your injuries, and a change of clothing. So come, Mr. Curtis. You need medical attention and clothing and shelter. And remember, Mr. Curtis, you entered Tibet without a visa."

"You spoke to Mr. Wilkins?"

"He provides no visa at all. you will answer to this violation of our laws. Tibet is rife with evacuees of China. Curtis was under arrest. The guards boxed him, and led him weakly, to the palace of the Princess.

At the princess' request, he was escorted to a neat bungalow not far from the palace which loomed like a large lamasery. He followed and was soon comfortable and fed opulently in a country so scarce of food.

Curtis was in the Chamberlain's charge after the testimony of the Chinese bandit. He got in touch by phone with Mr. Wilkins.

Curtis ate his meal although he was occasionally suspicious of an exotic pungency believing it might be poison. He did trust in the false oriental amiability on the Chamberlain and did not believe that Mr. Wilkins in his worldwide network of spies would save him without the gems. He cautiously did not expect to pass the night trapped in the bungalow waiting, for one, the Princess assassin. No sireee, at nightfall he would be on his way North further into the Himalayas and they could track him there if they chose, in the open among his friendly mountains. But he was in custody of the Chamberlain surrounded by his soldiers. A French doctor treated his injuries and refused to talk.

The Chamberlain returned with night clothes, silk pajamas and a bottle of French cognac to guarantee a solid night's sleep which Curtis gratefully accepted. The Chamberlain gave Curtis a present, an image of the Dalai Lama. He changed into the silk pajamas for the Chamberlain's satisfaction and slipped into his bed.

The Interrogation

THE PALACE OF THE Princess at Lhasa.

The palace room reeked of French perfume and jasmine dominating an oasis in the stench of the city.

The princess stood up from the silver-threaded divan, she was tall for a Tibetan woman, slim, moved with European grace and poise with the most expensive Parisian couture, in vintage, tight-fitting pants, and a gold spangled blouse. Her shoes were painted in gold leaf.

"That canaille, they believe they are modern. They are still possessed by demons. A planted prophecy from our astrologer will scare them out of their wits and drive them back into their devil ingested holes."

"I give orders today." confided the Chamberlain

"Depechez, and get reliable men we have used before in the other matters."

"By your leave."

"Go! Go!"

The ragged Chinese bandit lay prone on the carpet handing a large diamond to the Lord Chamberlain.

The princess lunged forward to see the diamond close up..

"Found in the hand of a foreigner. Three dead foreigners slain and one is still alive."

"Ah! Treasure of the Vedas. Do what you must."

"Well said," Chamberlain to a soldier. "Do you have the assassins ready?"

"Always on hand, Your Highness."

The Princess put her hands to her ears, "I don't want the details, you understand? Keep me informed at any hour. Then proceed."

"The Assassins? The Princess in her eagerness for the jewelry might be a mite indiscreet. This is, of course, a national secret and there could be a harsh reply from the Americans if they suspect a betrayal," said the Chamberlain to his aide.

"You know how women are. She is always bored. This may enliven her day."

"Discreet is the word. We are involved in international murder."

The Chamberlain laughed. "You speak to me of murder. It's another word for saintly Tibet."

The Chamberlain grinned, dismissed all, and assured the CIA chief by phone that he would act summarily to locate Mr. Curtis. No response to his phone call two days earlier about the disappearance of the crew.

Later, the Princess asked, "Did he mention the worth of the stolen jewelry?"

"Several millions and I believe we can multiply that ten hundred fold."

"One hundred million more than our state treasury."

"The Americans believe Tibetans are innocent of wealth and pray all day to get out of the rain."

"What further must we do, Chamberlain?"

Wilkins phoned.

Curtis a fugitive from American justice as Wilkins hinted? He was an embezzler who had stolen millions of dollars from a New York bank. That the authorities of Tibet should place him immediately under arrest and confiscate contraband gems and deliver them tout suite by plane to the USA, which he will immediately order from CIA.

The Chamberlain drummed fingers nervously. There was no time to lose. The assassins have orders to find the gems by torture or dissection of his body cavities.

The Parrot

A PARROT WAS HIS companion. He named him Agni, afer Agni, the mountain God. Curtis remembered an article about parrots in a nature journal. Parrots are the most intelligent birds of their species. Of course, they learn to speak languages of humans, are companionable pets. Moreover, they must be awarded and diverted, in the wild as in cages they seek puzzles and problems to solve. Without a problem or a puzzle to solve they become restless, tail to the bottom of the cage, lift their feathers, are depressed and die. For instance, the cage was a necessity for his parrot. It remained at the bottom of the cage and now waited on her perch waiting for the next problem. Curtis entwined a coin with a silk thread and gave it to her. She beaked it and went to work, squawking in pleasure. He wondered how soon this intelligent bird would be calling him, "Curtis."

In his confines, he had the company of a Macaw parrot with a powerful beak which he would poke through his cage for a caress on her plumed head, and she would croon with pleasure. He spoke vocally in several dialects. He and Ari the parrot ate the fruit that was served. He was enjoying the company of a pet, an animal love perhaps. The parrot loved him, he would gently peak his finger with his strong beak as a sign of affection.

Tiny lizards found a way into the room, and clung to the ceiling and walls in grotesque poses.

Once before he was confined and that happened at Bellevue. At that time he was overcome with a fear that puzzled him, freezes his bones and brain — now, with real fears, he felt fearless! He saw a dim meaning to his life, in all its daily confusion, the heading North.

Curtis took precautions about the exotic food served him. He was afraid of being drugged subtly to reveal the whereabouts of the treasure. It was possible, he thought, so he ate only fresh fruit untouched by syringe. In a sense he was being victimized by action. The action of the last few days, his muscles although bruised were alert, tense, ready by imminent act in itself. Never athletic, he was not athletic, his reflexes keen. So he hoped to avoid drugs that would seduce his mind and defeat his body.

"It is possible," he said to himself, "that actually, I am a lonely man, alone, except for a parrot" None in the world who loved him still. "An agent, and for whom?" He sensed the parrot's beak, and look into its sorrowful eyes. "Do you love me, parrot?"

As he was being led out he heard squawking, "Mr. Curtis."

The Assassins

THE DOOR WAS NOT locked. The assassins would have no need for a key that might alert the American. When the last grey of dusk disappeared, Curtis was out of bed, fully clothed in his wretched gear, his new paint box in a backpack securely on his back, the jewels in his crotch loined tightly. He left through a back window that led on to the main road. Why was he allowed to escape? He accepted the fact, the jewels! The Princess did not covet pieces of gems, but the Treasure itself. That could not be hidden on a person.

After a hundred feet or so, he sensed he was followed. He hid behind a demon pole and saw them, already daggers in hand, on his trail. He had no weapon but the frail easel, no good against these skilled killers with daggers and the garrote. He sprinted towards a lighted hut. They saw him and sprang after him. How or why, he was instantly garrotted by a thin steel wire that bloodied his neck with the first contact. The thin wire was wound around this standing pole that served as a clothesline for the inhabitants of the hut. The garrotte would kill him in time, but a time for the assassins to question him about the jewelry. An old woman whom he recognized as the dancer and the mother of the paralytic child he befriended, appeared to ask what was wrong. Curtis was gurgling like a skewed pig.

They seized the woman and threatened to kill her if he did not confess to the whereabouts of the gems. Then the abandoned cry of the frightened child. They signaled they will kill them both.

There was no growling, just a heavy huffing as the two hounds leapt on the assassins bearing them to the ground. They were working about biting at random at muscle in legs and arms, immobilizing the assassins. Then they dragged off the two into the bushes. Soon there was the sound of gnawing and the cracking of bones. The woman released the garrote and applied her shawl to the ringed wound. Curtis' first words were, "The dogs are eating them!" The woman signaled as if to say don't, they deserve their fate and the dogs deserved a hearty meal.

The Outrageous Demand of the Princess

BY THE TIME THE police arrived, crows and vultures had cleaned up left over carrion from the jaws of the hounds who were now back in their halters of the willow cart sleeping soundly along with the child. It was covered up in more ways than one. Curtis was found still bleeding on a bench in the Town park. The Chamberlain hurried to the scene and ordered the best medical attention at the French Hospital and expressed his apologies at this dangerous affront to an American citizen. He had already notified Mr. Wilkins of the death of his citizen and said there was no sign of jewels. Case closed, not quite. After a few days of first class medical attention at the hospital, Curtis was asked to attend a reception given by the Princess. While at the hospital Curtis took the two French doctors into his confidence and handed them the three jewels to have them monetized, deposited in a Swiss bank for the future needs of the hospital.

This time the throne room was bedecked with banners of decors like horrible tapestries, titantubularies of small drums and cymbals — a heavy pall of incense assured a ritual was expected that day.

That settled, until he heard from them again. He attended the reception in his honor which was extravagantly showy. The Princess sat alone on a throne like divan in a gown of some diaphanous silk, her lovely limbs could be seen and her breasts. He bowed.

"We shall see, Mr. Curtis. The Shaman has asked for your freedom in the hope that you will return the treasure. You may not be aware that I own it by inheritance, my blood is Aryan.

Curtis had the paint box in hand, although larger, it was light in weight, portable by two straps of damask silk. The brushes were pure bristle. He bowed grateful for the gift.

"And when you return from the mountain you will paint my clitoris." She spread her long legs revealing the clitoris studded with a diamond.

Curtis blinked, closed the lid of the paint box and raised his eyes to see the mischievous eyes of the Princess, and he lied, "I shall, your Highness."

"Then," the Princess sighed, "I shall be the envy of all Princesses and become the symbolic power of woman over man."

Curtis said, "I understand, your Highness."

The Lord Chamberlain interrupted — "It shall be a beautiful icon of a newer Tibet."

The Princess smirked.

The Palace

PICKED UP BY SOLDIERS, Curtis was brought to the palace. The Princess was seductively garbed in a one piece gown, split gracefully.

"The Lord Chamberlain advises me that you have lost your painting box, the loss gives you utter misery. I have asked the Lord Chamberlain to provide you with another." She clapped her hands. A servant appeared carrying a lacquered case of rare woods, opened to display brushes and tubes of paint.

"Mr. Curtis, the paint box is modeled after my jewel case, alas which is now empty and hopefully you will fill it with the mountain gems. Do you fancy it, Mr. Curtis?"

"Your Highness, it is admirable, and too generous."

"Yes, but imagine how generous you will be when you fill my jewel case."

"I have none of the gems, your Highness."

She said, "I greet our American visitor. He has been under the impression that we do not welcome him. This reception is a reminder how circumstances can be misunderstood. Is that apparent to Mr. Curtis?" her lips curled. She pointed to all the decorations.

"Yes, clearly, your Highness."

"Since I have honored you with this reception, you must honor me, Mr. Curtis."

"In whatever manner, your Highness."

She stepped down from the divan, laid apart her gown and stood naked before stepping down several steps to get closer to his person.

Curtis saw a brilliance in her pubic area. She came closer, not sure that he identified it and its location.

"It's a diamond. If you look closer it is attached to my clitoris. It is my formal gesture and mark of respect that you should paint my clitoris until I tell you to stop." The court leaned forward.

Curtis realized this was deadly amusement but he hazarded a quip, "Then the diamond is mine?"

She laughed dryly. "Will you won't you?"

"No Madam." She draped herself with the gown then said "You shall repay me for your major discourtesy by donating to the Royal House your possession of a quantity of jewelry. That will hardly match my matchless clitoris. Enough of the phallic worship."

Curtis knew he was in a hopeless situation and as a bravado said, "I shall paint your magnificent clitoris in color, your Majesty, when I return."

"Where are you going?"

"To the mountain."

No one dared laugh as the Princess grimaced cruelly. Curtis was doomed. "You are a criminal, Mr. Curtis. We shall execute you."

"This reception is a reminder how circumstances can be misunderstood."

"Is that apparent to Mr. Curtis?" her lips curled.

"Yes, clearly, your Highness."

At the moment of judgment as in a harum scarum movie serial, the Chamberlain signaled that Mr. Wilkins was on the phone, doubtful about the death of Curtis and the party, inquiring about the jewels.

"Where would you rather be? In my hands or in those of Mr. Wilkins?" The Princess asked.

"Yours, my Lady."

"Of course, Mr. Curtis, the Shaman has saved your life. He cast a spell over you to protect you. He believes you are a favored devotee of the mountain. However, we are still the civil authority, and the Chamberlain will keep an eye on you. When you return to exact our agreement to adorn my clitoris, my womanly being and the treasure.

We shall be vigilant. If you fail despite the pleas of the Shaman, you will feed the vulture. That is all! Let him go."

She smiled luminously closing her split gown. "Release the man."

The Shaman had arrived late to the court reception for Curtis riding his horse caparisoned white also with hideous designs, he rode to the upper stairs close to the divan of the Princess who did not give him a stare. The westernized woman thought him a court jester and a fool. He bowed his apologies then fell from his horse into a trance, trembling on the floor like a writhing lizard.

The Shaman writhed before the near or far proximity of Curtis, quivering like a cobra before a mongoose. All Shamanistic powers were a sham at a certain altitude where White Magic prevailed or Natural Magic, free of paranormal phenomena. Curtis would be close to power of cosmic energy in the form of the Kundalini of the mountains. The Kundalini or cosmic power that lay at the base of the mountain, and at the base of Curtis's spine. What the Shaman has seen in his spiritual assessment of the stranger was an unconscious adept, drawn by a natural kindness and compassion on a quest for God. His paintings were tremendous forces of concentration and meditation, unselfish. That gave him magic power and eventually the rise of his Kundalini which brought him upward and closer to a Godhead. Upward! North! The Catskills, the White Mountains, the Valleys of the Hudson and Mohawk, the Adirondacks, the Green Mountains, the Grand Himalaya. The Shaman's soul say he was born to God.

The Princess lingered for the result of the trance. She left trailing her gold threaded gown dreaming of a portrait of her jeweled clitoris painted by the handsome and daring very young American. Who know if done well enough and if propagandized it may renew the power and prestige of the clitoris so long over neglected by thousands of phallic worshipers. The Shaman rose with warning hands in the air.

"Do not harm the stranger. He has experienced Kundalini. He has siddhi and magical powers. He must not be deterred or the mountain Gods of Kundalini will avenge themselves upon us all, Princess!" But the Princess was gone behind draperies. "The treasure must not be violated again. Free him!" said the shaman.

If the Princess and part of her skeptical court considered his prediction and divinations as poppycock, the populace did not. They crowded the Shaman for more information about this stranger with a Shaman blessed destiny. And who achieved a partly, the summitry of Anari yoga, the cosmic power that arises from the base of the spinal column to liberation in a shower of diamonds in the last chakra in the forehead.

This the people knew from scripture and secret manuals on Tantra yoga. Where was this devotee of mountain gods? Where? so that they might kiss his feet and show him due veneration which the Princess and the court had not displayed. Woe to all, including the court if they showed no respect , an accepted devotee of the Mountain.

Painters

HE WAS BEING LED, it seemed north, as the trail grew steeper before him, the elders fell back and the young began gamboling among themselves. Their holiday was over but Curtis was not alone. Beside him was Hari, the sixteen year old hare-lipped cousin of the crippled girl in the wagon and the huge Tibetan mastiffs. He could not get rid of the stripling who vowed to his devotee. Curtis smiled, already among this maddening superstitious people, his one devotee, Hari. He was told by his girl cousin to guard him with his life for that would bring him eternal happiness and a kennel of Tibetan mastiffs all his own to command.

Curtis was short of some basic pigments, usually the ware of dyers everywhere. Tibet was notable for its dyed woolens and silks, harshly garish and flamboyant. Sometimes harshly crude, but in all colorations quite beautiful. He sought out a dyers shop and found one off a square. The shop was built square-like but with none of its matter of fact utilities. It was an effective sign post for the display of his dyers art, long banners crawling with serpents, solid red and blues that vied with the sky, silk cloth scintillating in sunlight and sultry at dusk. The dyer was either a showman or an artist.

Curtis rang a gong that resounded for half a minute before a Westernized Tibetan appeared at the door, bowed and waited for a request.

"You speak English, sir?"

"I do, sir. Not too well."

"Do you have red pigment to sell? And indigo?"

"We do, sir. How many pounds do you require of each?"

Curtis smiled. "Pounds, sir? I am not a dyer. I am a painter."

The Tibetan came closer to the counter. "Sir, what do you paint? Temples, churches?"

"None. I paint on canvas. I mix pigments with your dyes. I may have to dry them first then use a solvent in order to apply with a brush to a canvas or stone."

"Sir, I shall accommodate you as you wish. Color in pigment form or liquid as you wish. Although it is a rare request here. My father told me of the same request when he was younger from a person who called himself a painter. It is curious, he has good memory although he is very elderly man. Before I serve you willingly and gladly, may I introduce my father to you?"

"I would be pleased to meet him."

The young Tibetan retired to an inner room to return after a minute supporting a tottering veillard who squinted to adjust his sight to the sunlit awning. He spoke to his son who translated word for word. "My son, he looks like him. Many years ago a man, a non Tibetan who did not speak English but another language asked for the same color pigments which I granted willingly. He was tall like you, strong but he wore a beard which you don't. He was generous to me and respected our culture. I spoke to the sherpas who were his carrier when he climbed the mountains for days at a time. They were in awe of him. He sat for hours on a peak, painting in a lotus posture. One saw only that brush move unerringly across a wide canvas. With every brush stroke one heard a breath, like the mountain he was painting was breathing and alive. They said he was a Yogi. Although he wore no saffron gown." Then the old man began talking eagerly to his son, "Ask! ask him!" His son asked, "Are you by any chance the son of that man forty years ago?"

Curtis shook his head "I am sorry to disappoint your father's fond hopes, but I am not. I don't know the man you are referring to."

"But — but you follow his footsteps to the Himalayas as he did. You are a son in some respect."

The old dyer and pigment dealer, he understood Curtis' paintings at a glance, to be very much like that of his older white bearded predecessor who similarly impressed by not painting canvases really, but even to the dry, wrinkled eyes of the old connoisseur, each painting was a deep meditation. It was not a mantra, as one to be gazed upon, to tour consciousness. Through painting it was the ultimate praxis of mediation, nothing static, a step forward, a lesson completed, another in the offing as rigorous as the mountain practices of Yoga. But the old man did not think that the young man, differently to an older and wiser man of fifty years ago, he would realize the deepest psychological gift given to a human being, in a painting. The old dyer, his pale lips with chagrin at the absence of paintings. But one small canvas, a study from the pickings of Hari would confirm his elevated opinion of the artists. The old man would never know what was in common between the paintings of the young man and the older.

Would he discover the body corpse of the former painter — visitor of years past. An Alpine flower?

"From what you tell me, old man, I should like to be him."

"But you are, you are sir," the old man insisted, spittle rising at his lips in his trembling vehemence.

"Old man, what happened to him since you say I stand in his shadow?"

"He remained all summer. Climbed all peaks or most and produced paintings which he shipped back to foreign lands. Then he disappeared, some sherpa said he left for Mongolia, others said he died on a peak. That is not true because a few months after his disappearance, our telegrapher heard from him, a bit of money he thought he owed me."

"Are you a worshiper of mountain Gods, my father asks?"

"What did your father, old friend say when asked the same question?"

He said, "I paint mountains."

The Shaman

WAS TIBET A SPIRITUAL place of superstition, filth, cruelty, demonology, of decay? It existed unmindfully of any purpose but to be beautiful? Ah! Beauty!

The Shaman is wrong. What made Curtis so circumspicious as a man? He was a painter of sorts, from New England, a former member of disowned religion. What was so special? That he was virginal? for the Shaman to accept his privacy? Art? Beauty was a wonder?

A revered mountain in the Himalayas, a long precipitous climb from the palace he was soon surrounded by the prayerful who kissed his feet, offered him beggar alms. All they had were morsels from their own mouths. Mothers brought him infants to bless. Curtis could do nothing but remain immobile trying his best to look benign. Soon the Shaman arrived on foot, terribly upset, his face in tears, his metal bars jangling.

The Shaman fell to his knees. He groveled, ate dirt. Importuned forgiveness in loud cries to heaven towards the mountain, K. He shambled ahead, clearing the way for the devotee on his way, K. where he hope the devotee would implore forgiveness on his behalf to the mountain God. He crouched begging minor mountain Gods to come to his aid. Curtis felt sorry for the anguished old man and handed him a tiny brush with which he was cleaning his teeth. The Shaman accepted it which a whoop and rolled on his stomach with joy.

Satisfied by the Shaman expiation by the token gift of the brush, his followers also rolled on the ground with joy. They had been delivered of punishment by the mountain God who possessed five peaks at his command. Who could stop the monsoon? Drive mudslides into villages, avalanches? Raging tempests that tore hair out of your skull, could darken the sky for month destroying sunlight and the crops they feed on. Oh, what a deliverance they lifted the Shaman to his saddle and kissed his boots.

The clangor ritual bells and banging of pots herald his appearance as he climbed higher. Others were on hand to greet him, offering him water to drink. Mountain villagers beholden flocked to serve him food and assistance, and several offered pretty winsome wives. And a threshed bed to lie on. On huge boulders he was effigies of Kundalini and then in subsidiary positions the four minions of Kundalini. The mighty mountain in the opinion of the Tibetans was more sacred than Everest.

He might say the effigies painted on stone and sometimes carved were not pleasant to look at, as a matter of fact they were tearful. But he knew the Tibetans well now. They demonized heaven and earth, why? On the other hand, mountains gave him a sense of Majesty, nothing in the configurations of the peaks and canyons that the mountains were hiding devils. These ignorant tribes accepted him in his Western garb of a yogi and not a climber. No saffron robes and amulets around his neck.

He was hungry so they stopped for tea and a piece of cheese and honey. A convenient told him the height of the rock on which they were sitting was four thousand feet. Curtis did not feel an actual shortness of breath but he was lunged out by Hari's pace who was in a hurry to go somewhere. He turned his head upward, but was only a glimpse between two gangly towers of sheer grey granite. Between the two peristyle towers he saw the peak, an interminable peak rising into what appeared to be a steel blue vault.

Yet Curtis' heart, that telltale heart was clean. He had no doubts he was no worthless infidel to any truth. This Kundalini, the Shaman spoke about. Yes, he recalled an incident a week after he tripped the bandits to deaths in the gorge, when he had a fit of violent trembling, shock waves were coursing up his spine, like electrical jolts, which then subsided and he felt a superior strength and he thought predictive powers, he was never actually afraid at the court and the possible consequences of Mr. Wilkins and the Chamberlain illicit conspiracies. Silly, he imagined the mountain would crash down upon them. Was it the end of a long voyage that began with meeting a ragtag of pimply adolescents in a Greenwich Village bar. His knees buckled and he gave obeisance in the Tibetan fashion to the looming mountain peak, Hari followed suit, afraid he would miss out on a puppy.

He was crying but his tears were scorched by a rising high velocity wind whipping across the little plateau that was left before the really arduous climb upwards. Hari adeptly rubbed a kind of smelly lard on his face and hands to prevent burns that were difficult to heal. Trees were thinning and songs of birds very distant. Kundalini, he cried aloud which was not understood by Hari who was eating lard out of the ointment jar which he found tasteful. Dear Kundalini, my driving force tell me. Give me the strength to survive the sublimity of the mountain. And the Himalayas. I thought of dying, my heart fails, my fingers are turning cyanotic and blue. After all my unconscious traveling, will I be worthy of your presence?"

At night, Hari huddled closer to Curtis in his meager tent space. Outside the mountain Gods were talking among themselves. Deep in valleys and on tops of peaks, in the low lying meadowland, shined like gigabits butterflies, flashes of electronic action in purple, blue, and red, thin as paper lanterns but so large. Electronic fires flared, moved, swarming over the magnetized stone. In the meadowlands, they shone like will of the wisps. At dusk a finished painting was suddenly illuminated by one of these globular glows. Curtis extended his hand to save the painting, why? But he did, he felt no burning, just a static playing on his hand and a slow dim out with no scorch on the paint. The stone painting fell apart as if pulverized and only dust stirred where it stood once. Hari looked into the man's face to see astonishment or a reaction but there was none. But from then on, his paint was incisive on stone.

Hari on the heels of Curtis held no fears at the destination of his man. His girl cousin told him a man to be revered, her Tibetan mastiffs of like opinion. Hari was honored to hold paint box, the palette steady in the brisk winds, oftentimes the brush strokes moved by whim of the existing wind. Whatever evolved on the stone plates painted peaks and valleys he bowed reverently even as he jettisoned them. Too heavy to carry forward in the thinning enervating air. Each painting a step-stone leading upwards to a resting place of which he did not have a surmise. Soon no more canvas. Hari was told to gather flat stone as the new canvas. Every time a gorgeous stone left his hand to lay discarded on an escarpment, Hari wept.

Remembrance

FIVE DAYS OF THE CLIMB

CURTIS BIT HIS TONGUE when he was moved to explain, or describe by metaphor what he was experiencing in the mountains. Artists, he remembered could move the universe with a metaphor. But life to Curtis was not a metaphor. Not a poetic conceit, but a substantive value beyond measure, something as solid as the mountain ahead of him, pure consciousness. How far can his paintings probe? He was now painting on shards and scrabbles of laminated granite.

Curtis realized that he himself even here in this supreme seclusion was subject to fancy of his mind. How to distinguish his new rational or super thinking from hallucinations or the blue flamed images of the long, tantalizing view. It was too confusing for him as he grappled with the sharp ledges and bruising stone of the upward climb. He deliberately hurt himself as if clarifying dream induced visionary horizons. If he were halfway omniscient of why he was climbing the folding mountains were designs of origami. Occasionally there was falling of heavy pollen from a grove a thousand feet below that marched like an oriflammes across the valley. What, what did it all mean? Better to fall twenty eight thousand feet mountain free to his death?

Mornings were fulminations of colors like looking into a magical heartstone. One morning Hari preparing hot tea pitched forward and fell. Hardly breathing, Curtis gave him his breath for fifteen minutes, then told the revived to return. The air was too rarefied for his tiny lungs. Hari protested but was glad to leave even without his puppy mastiffs.

He was told on the sly by the Dyer's son to bring back something of his master. His arms were empty.

On every path and near and far rolling meadow lay a green velvety carpet, speckled in yellow and blue poppies, large leafed roses, fairy like anemones, on hardier round the surprising beauty of the prickly thistle, trailing columbine, and eglantine primroses. The flowers caught the attention of the eye, not of the nose. Despite an enhancing blow, the fragrances were mild. No need perhaps to lure insects at that height. Why didn't Curtis stop to paint these rare curiosities. His eyes were blind to either side, he looked up front at the mountain surface.

Curtis did not know how to prepare himself for the loneliness and solitude the absence of Hari would provoke. A thousand feet higher he searched for the ambling talk of the hare-lipped Hari's lips. As he climbed higher emboldened by a power he did not recognize, he lost that sense of solitude that make all indifferent to your fate. There was an increasing end, of fulfillment that displaced solitude or its need. Rich oxygen now surrounded him making him more confident of his purpose. In his eagerness he over-drank the oxygen and began to hallucinate. He was back among the Beatniks listening to Cassady in a brilliant impromptu. He saw Jack Kerouac and Holmes in a harmony of poems. Susan's fingers attempted to open his fly. His mind cleared. Dreyfus dancing, a spiritual binge they called it. He assumed a Lotus posture and regained the appropriate rhythmic breathing level and resumed his climb.

Back in town, Hari was seized by the Princess' police. She personally questioned about Curtis. Was he alive? Dead? What did he do in the mountains, paint? Only? The gems? What sorcery did he devise to destroy her with the help of the mountain God? Hari's tongue was helpless. He only told him honestly what he knew. Went empty handed up to Dyer without an easel. Officials at Potal scanned the mountain slopes and peaks for sight of Curtis but he was lost in the clouds. Wilkins too, despite all the mangled message he got from the Palace of Potal assigned an agent in Nepal to collect notices of Curtis death or disappearance.

Rare is the Air

ANOTHER THOUSAND FEET UPWARD he could not ward his eyes of what was before him. If you closed your eyes, then opened them you saw the loggia, the balcony, and mezzanine and the foyer of the Paris Opera House! It was an espalier to the wonders of mists. Immediately Curtis saw his paint was no match for the rampant beauty of the moist extravagant colors. Curtis was spell bound and almost forgot his mountains lay ahead. But a hushing reminded him of the lateness of the hour. Among the ranks of the distant space he thought he saw a snow leopard.

Efflorescence remained in his eyes and when he faced the bare blue of a mountain, the colors to imprint themselves, little tattoes.

Horned hooves of the families of Himalayan goats left no trail, there was no distinct hoof to be seen by snow leopard or a hunter leaving an airy scent or a spoor as the goats leaped from crag to crag.

He now saw only shadows of himself, no reflections. The blue was deeper by the day, at times almost indigo or bright purple but would revert to blueness once more. Curtis! Are you happy? How do you feel? Ecstatic? Rhapsodic? Drunk? A stone that moves? His hands were bloodied by the stone, muscles stringy like jerky, all fat gone. If he could talk with his burned lips he would say, I am at the end of a string as his breathe weakened.

There was a transparency in the atmosphere near and far that appeared to cleanse his mind of all stray thoughts as if there was an involution to another self.

At eight thousand feet that self was breathing in a stressful fashion. He quaffed more tea.

Curtis huddled in a small tent which riffed all night and the air became less breathable. Pains ranged throughout the muscles of his chest and diaphragm.

Curtis was prepared to die breathless somewhere above him on a crag or fall to a large crevasse. He struggled another thousand feet upward. How was he? He fell on his back, the blue sky, a deeper blue. A rainbow was rising from a mist in a nearby canyon. He had a gruesome thought. A fear that haunted him ever since he set foot in Tibet that the vultures would eat him as carrion. Not here, at this height. He will become just another small wreckage of living carbon and limestone and myth. He was not at peace. He was numb.

The Mountain

THE MOUNTAIN

He was dying!

Nonetheless a warmth feeling.

"Mr. Curtis!"

"Who? I? Curtis?"

"I am Agni, the messenger."

A swoop of oxygen jolted his lungs. Breathing! He was breathing again! His jaws moved. He was below the peaks. How?

"Agni, of Agni Yoga, my yoga as the Shaman said?"

"Precisely."

"I can't. I can't see your face."

"Mr. Curtis, as a painter you may be disappointed. No faces or portraits on these peaks."

"I have a face, I am Curtis. You know me, how else?"

"You are dazed by the oxygen. You will feel better higher up. Clearer."

"Up? I see I failed you. I did not reach the peak on my own. You saved my life."

"You reached one peak of the five."

"How?"

"Now Curtis, you have been unaware of our assisted ascent. We are now on the peak, we have been moving, but that is not the beyond, a step more perhaps. Indulge your Messenger for a moment. Imagine you and I are standing on a bridge over a strong running river."

77

"Yes, I am standing on a wooden bridge looking down into a swollen stream."

"What do you see?"

"Oh! Dear Messenger, what delights you give me. How wonderful! I see a parade, bands, banners floating, singing, dancing, great feasting and bulging cathedrals. Long pilgrims, dear happy faces of my childhood and friends. They are waving to me. There go my canvases all in order, thousands going by. A blazon of colors give me this vision of the plain lands and return me to the world of colors. Thank you kind heart, dear Messenger. I feel better."

"Come closer to the edge, Curtis." Curtis was ecstatic! The center of five majestic mountains like planetary bodies. He is a pauper. Why try to describe it? Painter? He is no writer, poet. A tremendous flash, there appeared from the mouth of a deep canyon deep down below, a rising whirling girasole of an infinity of colors.

Iridescences, that could not resist independence or primaries, that too dissipated in hues and tints, never before seen by Curtis. Curtis searched at his feet. "Where, where is my brush? My paint box?" I must get this on canvas, stone, or my palms! He was at the edge perilously close to falling, his brush flailing the space. Paint spilling over his feet. Color was fleeting, moving, stand still a moment, a second, an ion of time but the whirling girasole becoming more brilliant, more coruscating in fiery reds. It passed over Curtis' figure, commanding his brush, threatening to put the entire display into a paint pot. When the girasole now illuminated the pitiful figure of Curtis at the edge of the peak threatening to put the display into his paint box if it did not stay. Curtis thrashed himself to the ground and lay still.

"Mr. Curtis, the stream on the river bottom is stagnant and lethargic in its flow, it is life's tedium, the every day diurnal sameness, the boredom, the ennui! That is closer to death, you must endure to stay alive, create, and culture, itself.

"Boredom! Mr. Curtis, it is not possible your hope. No hope without creativity! Which makes life stir from the smallest cell imaginable. You don't wish to be mind in that flow, you leave so far. The artist in man transforms it, overcomes its apathy, and despair. Men are born in ignorance, they fashion tools to learn. You have your brush." Curtis rose.

"Curtis, color is not the beyond, neither is the peak."

"Cannot exist any longer. Allow me to die, food for vultures. My brush fails me."

"You have lost something precious to you."

"Yes, the lovely earth. In Springtime, color?"

"Now Curtis let's be fair — back to the bridge."

Curtis got up meagerly. "Yes, yes to my friends. My canvases. Earth! Color."

Curtis looked down into the river, no sodden discolored canvases, tolling bells for millions dead, nuclear blasts that reduce color to brown dust, phlegm, suppurations, man killing man.

A grey mold seeped through all the carnage and misery, the slush of rotting flesh.

Curtis cried out, "Enough! Enough!"

"Curtis, we only have to walk along the embankment to follow a crystal river."

A crystal river appeared.

"Thank you, dear Messenger. My heart hurts."

"Not the air. You were affected by human river. There will be a balm, I promise."

"Thank you, dear Messenger."

"I deserve the sanctity?"

"You dedicated your heart and soul in depicting, rather understanding logically through your painting the manifestations of this spirit through the sublimity of its peaks. You are kindly, even with the misguided and hapless Beatniks who feared for God. You discovered in your paintings, your brush probed the most arcane secrets of a presence. Your family earned moral credits. The first brush in your fingers pointed you to a Quest."

"What you see is only illustrative to your perfect state of will, there are other languages, other conveyances of communication of which one not yet participant. Your ego is language talking to itself. You will be accustomed to a language which is pure understanding.

A place of no metaphors, all things are themselves, and cannot be learned except by art. Constant, the Vedas, that ancient Eastern philosophy was a psychological process inherent in all mythologies — if you are tied to a star, man moves as a North star.

His compulsive painting, the trail of which is along the Appalachians, the Adirondacks, Catskills, Green Mountains, and the Himalayas were creative efforts to understand himself.

He learned panel by panel, canvas and canvas, stone face and marble slabs, by memories of an artist's experience.

All the props of this experience were symbolizing a deeper understanding of himself, by his brush.

What was the ensuing silence of the mountains but a hushed aspiration of beauty, as in the artist's work of art.

There are cooperative moments of ecstasy which was transitional. What is painting through a mirage? His intoxication with color was a love to a more permanent palette. Yes, he was still a Beat, thinking like one, an experimental expectation of youthful life.

"Nothing is his palette, perhaps. As I said, I am a figure of a vast imagination, I speak with restraint." The Messenger said.

"Perhaps I don't recognize realizations achieved within myself. I don't wish to be disarming. I don't think of myself as a monk or a pilgrim. I conceive of myself as a painter, as an artist not as a God-serving monk. There were times I thought I was driven by those demonic powers that afflict artists, where they sacrifice lives before the outstretched arms of beauty." He was God's naif following instructions, given a marked path or given by a school child to trace.

Still a Beatnik!

"Not a silly thought, Curtis. You are a heroic Beatnik."

Curtis shows signs of panic, "I must live with color!!"

"The beyond loves color as eagerly as you do. It created color which as you know is not just white light."

"I know, I know! But can't it be an everlasting color wheel?"

"So many questions when you are on the doorstep."

So he was, realized Curtis thought. For they had risen gradually during the conversation.

Curtis flailed out with his arms seeking a grip on a stone from which he could make his descent. Stone pulverized in his hands. "I am sorry dear Messenger. Do with me what you like. I cannot leave the earth while it still possesses color!"

"But the earthy does not last. You saw."

"As long as it lasts."

"I see the artist is ascendant."

"I wish to die among colors."

"Consider yourself an orphan who has been adopted."

"Yes!"

"Mr. Curtis don't play the simpleton. You painted his surfaces and peaks for he is the Lord of all Mountains, more venerated than his brother, Mt. Everest, the Lord of the Himalayas. You chose well..."

"I chose?"

"Instinctively."

Above his head Curtis felt the scythe of a lamination of a blue steel wind that whined, then desisted.

Curtis was not aware if he was sitting or standing in the glutinous darkening. The Messenger was a faint visage near him.

"Where? The spirit of what it represents, what it is, the holiest spirit that graces the universe. Towering above all its brother mountains."

He placed a large slab of rock between his legs to set it upright and gazed at his work for the last time. He now saw something that he recognized in everything he is, a vibrant and often a faint arteriole of color, a river, a gully, a crevasse, a mountain, smaller mountains, a deep valley. In all there was this blood-like line directed always upward. Often it fumed fiery or became a faint glow, a standing beacon or a road directional. Always upward and higher. Now it glowed like a huge pharos and now the conduits ended in red heat of a giant kiln at 28,000 feet.

He was free of the gibbering Shaman. He was led by Agni, the God of fire, a spirit, a figment of all imagination. The hail of fire ended and his life in wind drift ashes, "Take my hand!" Curtis intoned in the vast silence.

"Remember, sublimity, sincerity of all things, and fullness of nothing."